# WereC

Ian Fc

A guy in the middle of the theater was c                         straw
in his oversized soda, trying to get the wate                     of ice.
Even though the house lights had come up,                        ome
guy with thinning hair and entirely too much enthusiasm
morning.

Stanley loved the movie *Con Air* as much as anyone. It's why he was watching a Nic Cage triple feature after midnight on a Sunday night when he had to work the next day. But he couldn't abide someone clapping in a theater.

*Who's that applause for?* Stanley wondered. Nic Cage? He wasn't in the theater. None of the filmmakers were. And he was ninety percent sure there wasn't even a projectionist in the booth. The movie just sort of ran on its own. It was weird behavior. Then again, that's why he showed up.

Nic Cage fans were weird. And Stanley Miller was a serious Nic Cage fan. He was okay with the weirdness. It came with the territory. It made spending nearly six hours straight watching *Mandy, Face/Off,* and *Con Air* seem entirely reasonable.

The clapper ended his round of applause and stood up. He shuffled out of the theater along with everyone else. Stanley made sure his soda was finished and then joined the small but respectable crowd.

The town had Cage Fever, and it was one of the first times in years Stanley had been truly excited. A production crew had just been on location for about a month filming a new Nic Cage movie. Stanley had tried out to be an extra, but his manager at Gates' Market had never seen the brilliance in Nic Cage's work and was thus unmoved by Stanley's pleas for time off.

Stanley dropped his empty cup in the recycling on the way out of the theater and hit the street. It was a warm night, and he was glad for it since he'd walked there and now needed to walk home. If he cut through the park, he'd shave a good half hour off of his time. Plus, he'd get to enjoy the park, which is something he always told himself he needed to do but never actually got around to doing. Enjoying parks was a very adult thing to do and so he would do it. At one in the morning.

Kids enjoyed parks and then old, responsible people enjoyed them and Stanley was somewhere in the middle. He worked too much and then was too lazy in his down time and never really had park time. Time to just be in nature like a woodsperson.

There had never been a movie filmed in town before and it was very exciting. They'd closed off a big chunk of downtown for a whole week and even though he wasn't an extra, he did get to watch a car chase from the sidelines in which Nic Cage's stunt double nearly got exploded by Frank Grillo's stunt double. It was intense.

The park smelled like dog farts and trees. The grass was wet with dew and it soon soaked the canvas of his shoes, leaving his feet oddly slimy. He no longer wanted to be a woodsperson, but it was saving him time, at least.

No wind blew through the trees of the park, and the sky was clear. The moon was a silver orb, lighting his way from birch to pine to oak and then through open fields of grass.

By the time he got to bed, it'd be after two, he was sure. He'd end up feeling exhausted at work the next day. On the upside, all he had to do was stock the dairy section of the store and if he didn't stack yogurt with a lot of gusto, no one was likely to care. His job made no difference at all in the grand scheme of the world and, in all honesty, he liked it that way.

There was a time when he was a boy and thoughts of being an astronaut or a firefighter filled his head. Now both of those things seemed exhausting and terrifying in equal measure. If an astronaut screwed up at work, they could explode throughout the atmosphere and rain down across an entire hemisphere. If a firefighter screwed up, the entire city of Chicago could burn down. That actually happened once. He read about it on the internet.

For Stanley's money, Nic Cage was a superior hero. He could solve world class problems in under two hours, whether that involved stealing the Declaration of Independence or drop kicking ladies who raised honey bees. Failing that, there were real astronauts and real firefighters in the world. They were all doing a good job, it seemed. Things got along just fine with Stanley where he was. And, in turn, those firefighters and spacemen got to have fresh yogurt on a regular basis. The world kept on turning.

The sound of his own footsteps was the only sound in the park and for several long minutes, he trudged along, listening to the damp squish and making it like a song in his head. It was only when he crossed one of the park's many bike paths and he saw a quarter reflecting the moonlight that he noticed something was off.

Stanley stopped in his tracks. He couldn't think of a single thing in the world that still cost a quarter, but he wasn't about to leave it sitting on the ground. And that's when he heard the squishing sound of footsteps in the damp grass that were no longer his own.

He turned and looked back the way he had come. Several yards back, a man in a dark jacket was following in Stanley's footsteps. Stanley turned away quickly, as though looking at the man was some kind of grievous sin, as though he were peeping at him illicitly. He left the quarter where it was and kept walking.

The park was large and there was no reason to think there wouldn't be other people walking around in it. Maybe this stranger was heading to the same part of town Stanley was. Maybe he'd just come from the film festival as well. Anything was possible. There was no reason to suspect anything bad was happening. No reason at all.

The certainty that the stranger was stalking Stanley was the only thought in his brain. Sure, he could have just been out for a walk. But what if he wasn't? Stanley started walking faster.

He tried to keep his increased pace still casual. It wasn't a run, not even a mall walking speed. But faster than his normal speed. It was a hustle. Just a casual, late night park hustle that was sending fear pheromones into the night. He'd laugh about it when he got home, safe and sound.

The stranger began a fear-free hustle as well. Stanley was certain it was a prank now. Or maybe the other person was wearing very flimsy shoes and was distraught that they had absorbed so much dew and now needed to hurry home. There could have been a million reasons for them to be matching his speed and direction in the middle of the night. A million and one, even.

Stanley broke into a run. As much as he wanted to convince himself that the dark stranger was just an innocent traveler in the night, his own mind refused to believe itself. The stranger was a mad strangler, a late-night stabber of pedestrians, or some kind of blood-thirsty former surgeon who would remove Stanley' spleen and make him eat it.

There had never been a time in Stanley's life when he'd been praised for his running prowess. Athleticism was as foreign to him as New Zealand was. He had run before, in much the same way he'd once seen Niagara Falls. It was a thing that had happened in his past. But he gave it his all in that moment.

Blood pumped through his veins so loudly he could hear it in his ears. He puffed and wheezed as his lungs took in great gasps of night air. He was not out of shape necessarily, but nor was he in shape, either. He was tall and thin and lacked muscle tone or stamina in any appreciable quantities. But he did have adrenaline, and that was something.

The sound of his own feet mixed with his thundering pulse and then another sound. Pursuit. The stranger was running as well.

"I don't have any money!" Stanley yelled into the dark. "I don't have anything!"

He made it across the grass to another walking path and took a sharp right, his feet slapping along the pavement as he ran towards the edge of the park. He could see the exit and the streetlights beyond in the distance, and his fear mixed with a tentative sense of relief. Safety was within reach. Surely, his maniac stalker would never dare follow him into the light.

His feet smacked on the ground and a moment later, he realized it was the only sound in the park. Stanley swallowed his own fear and did the unthinkable as he ran - he looked backward.

No one was there. The stalker had vanished into the night, no doubt scared off by the impending street lights and the protective power against murder they provided. He was safe.

He laughed, very quietly and with more strain than he would have liked in his winded condition. It was nothing. It was probably just some stupid kid. He was fine.

Stanley slowed, his heart still racing, but with a sense of relief coming over him. He was very near the exit now and would be home in minutes.

The figure stepped out of the bushes ahead of him on the path, and Stanley screamed. It was not as manly a sound as he would have liked, breathy and too high pitched. He stopped in his tracks, ready to flee in the opposite direction with whatever limited energy he could muster to keep running. And then his eyes widened, and he froze in place.

No street light was nearby to cast its protective glow over Stanley and his dark pursuer, but the light of the full moon bathed the man's face in a silver white glow, glinting off the earrings he wore, that might as well have been the noonday sun. The distinctive hairline, the long nose, the tight smile. He would have recognized that face anytime and anywhere.

"Nic Cage?" Stanley said. Nicolas Cage's smile widened ever so slightly.

"I saw you and you saw me. Don't pretend like you don't know who I am, girly man," Cage replied. Stanley opened his mouth to respond and then stopped short, unsure of what to say to that.

"It's like we're on two different channels now," Cage added. Stanley ran a hand through his hair.

"Wow. This is... I'm such a fan. I just came from a film festival of your movies and you're... chasing me through a park."

Cage nodded, his smile as intense as Stanley would have expected it to be. In the moonlight, he looked a little too much like some of his less stable characters. Stanley's heart was racing a mile a minute, coming down off the high of the chase and then rising to a new high of meeting arguably his favorite actor of all time.

"What's that like?" Cage asked. "Describe it like Hemingway."

Stanley rubbed the back of his head. He'd been a fan of Nicolas Cage since he was about ten years old and he watched *The Rock* with his dad. They saw *Con Air* and *Face/Off* the next day and he was sold. When his parents split up a few years later, he'd watch a Nic Cage movie every weekend he spent with his dad. And when his father died of cancer shortly after Stanley got his own place, he had left him his St. Christopher's medallion on a silver chain, an old tuxedo, and every Nic Cage movie he owned on both VHS and DVD or Blu-ray. It was a formidable collection.

He couldn't think of Nic Cage without thinking of his dad, and that made him happy. Not that his father had been anything like Nic Cage, but the connection stretched back years in his mind and was carved in stone. Nic Cage made him feel safe, as weird as that was. And now he was standing in front of him in a park at night, spouting something close to gibberish. It was the best possible way they could have met.

"It's nice?" Stanley said, trying to answer Cage's question. He had never read Hemingway and had no idea how the man would describe anything.

"Right. Well, you'll be seeing a lot of changes around here," Cage said then, taking a step towards Stanley. "Papa's got a brand new bag."

Stanley frowned. He recognized the line. He'd just heard it in the theater.

"Are you quoting -" he began. Cage grabbed his wrist before he could finish the question and yanked him forward, nearly pulling his arm from the socket. The man's grip was like iron and he was strong, ridiculously strong.

Stanley stumbled and let out a startled cry as Nic Cage pulled him close. The actor's other arm circled around his back as though the two were suddenly dancing. He could smell Cage's sweat and a faint hint of something perfumey and, for an instant, the two of them were literally cheek to cheek.

"What's happening?" Stanley whispered, his voice cracking. Cage didn't answer. Instead, he lowered his head and pain erupted in Stanley's shoulder. Nic Cage bit him.

He felt the man's teeth sink into the base of his neck, just above the shoulder. It was like being crushed at first until his teeth penetrated through the material of his shirt and finally his flesh, pushing his father's chain into the wound as he did so.

Stanley screamed and then Cage shook his head, screaming as well as he pulled away. Blood ran down the man's chin and Stanley felt like he was on fire. He pushed Cage away and stumbled back, falling on his ass off of the edge of the path next to a tree.

Cage shrieked and wiped at his own face. Wild, crazy eyes fixed on Stanley and he lunged like an animal. Stanley reached out, patting the ground in a desperate panic, and felt something dry and hard under his right hand. He gripped and swung, sending a tree branch in a wide arc that clipped Cage across the side of the head and knocked him away.

Momentum and a lack of preparedness proved to be too much for Nic Cage and he was sent off balance, falling to the path as Stanley got to his feet.

"What the hell, Nic Cage?" he yelled, holding a hand to his shoulder. Cage hissed at him as he rolled over, reaching for Stanley's shoe. Fear and anger spurned him onward and Stanley kicked Cage in the face before turning to run, making his way to the streetlights and the safety he needed them to provide.

"Listen, I think we got started on the wrong foot!" Cage yelled after him. Stanley's shoulder throbbed and he could feel blood running down his back and his chest. "It doesn't matter how far you run! There are some demons you can't escape!'

Stanley did not look back. He followed the path out of the park and then ran down the street several blocks towards his apartment. He could feel his cell phone in the pocket of his jeans and a voice in his head told him over and over to call the police, but he couldn't stop. Nic Cage was going to eat him if he stopped. No one would ever believe a word of it. He had to get home. He'd figure out what to do when he got home.

Air conditioner compressors and buzzing lights and distant cars all filled the night with the background music of life. But he heard no more shouts from Cage and heard no more footfalls. He refused to look back, though, convinced that Cage's maniacally smiling face would be bobbing along right behind him if he did so.

He reached his apartment and struggled in his pocket to get the keys out. His hand was slick with his own blood and sweat. He cursed and paced in place at the apartment door. No sounds followed him, but he couldn't turn around. He couldn't look back.

The door unlocked with a click and he slipped into the building, turning for the first time as he locked it behind himself and looked out at the street through the door's window. The sidewalk was empty; the street was empty.

His breath was still coming in deep, panicky gasps. He made his way through the apartment lobby to the elevator and took it up to the third floor, where he shared an apartment with his roommate Cameron.

The lights were off as he stumbled into the apartment. He felt like his heart was going to explode out of his chest. Pain shot from his shoulder through his entire body. His head throbbed as though there were some sort of engine pulsing inside of it.

Stanley made his way awkwardly past the kitchen and down the hall to his bedroom. Cameron was likely still awake, but his door was closed and he didn't want to disturb him. He couldn't explain what had happened and didn't want to. He wanted to take care of his shoulder and just sleep.

His bedroom door closed with a click, and he locked it, looking around the dark room. Moonlight streamed in his window, giving it a soft glow, and he stumbled to his bathroom, turning on the light and grimacing.

Blood soaked his shirt all the way to the waist. Cage must have hit an artery or something. He wondered if he was losing too much blood, if he was at risk of dying. How could he die from a Nic Cage bite? What kind of obituary would someone write for that?

He gritted his teeth and gasped as he pulled his t-shirt over his head, sending new waves of terrible pain through his arm, chest, and back. He tossed the blood and sweat soaked garment on the floor and looked at himself in the mirror. The bite was as clear as day, dark red teeth marks sunk deep into his flesh and forced inside right along with them the silver chain his father had given him. Cage's teeth had pushed it into the wound.

With a scream he muffled against the towel on the bathroom door, Stanley pulled the silver chain from the bite on his shoulder. He heard a faint hiss, and the wound sputtered and fizzed as though peroxide had been poured on it. His head swam, and he felt like he might throw up.

The mirror of his bathroom was spattered with water spots and a splash of dried toothpaste spray he'd been meaning to clean up for over a week. He stared at the wound on his shoulder, the still-flowing blood and the distinctly outlined tooth indentations. Then he passed out.

# Chapter Two

The taste of bathroom linoleum steeped in saliva woke Stanley up. He opened his eyes and pushed himself up awkwardly, spitting into the pool of drool in which he'd been sleeping.

There was dried blood on the floor and he felt like someone had beaten him six shades of stupid. His shoulder hurt, his head hurt, and everything else hurt as well. He got to his feet slowly and looked at himself in the mirror.

The bags under his eyes were dark and tinged purple around the edges. His chest and shoulder and arm were covered in dark flakes of dried blood. He stared at the wound on his shoulder and blinked. The outline of Nic Cage's teeth was clearly visible. But they were puffy and inflamed now, swollen closed and oozing blood and clear fluid. It looked like a wound that had happened days in the past and was becoming infected.

Stanley turned on the tap and wet his hand, rubbing water across the wound. The rehydrated blood ran thin and red down his chest and shoulder. He rubbed more water in, cleaning the bite as well as he could. The scabby bits peeled away, revealing pink, puckered flesh under each one. A perfect set of Cage teeth, top and bottom above his collarbone.

Only a pair of punctures were still open, the ones that had been inflicted by Cage's canine teeth. They had not sealed up from the swelling as the rest had, and each one oozed a thin, sticky fluid that was not blood at all.

Stanley tried to wash the wound, wincing at the stinging sensation that the soap caused as he worked it into the small punctures, then dried it off on his hand towel. The skin was red and angry. He frowned at it. Nicolas Cage had bitten him. It looked like it would need antibiotics. He had a Nic Cage mouth infection.

"Goddammit," he muttered. What was he supposed to do about that?

Stanley used some toilet paper to try to clean up the floor and tossed the wet, bloody clumps into the toilet. The urge to call the police was there, but what was he supposed to say? Nicolas Cage bit him in the park? They'd think he was either a liar or crazy.

He left the bathroom for the bedroom, where he changed his clothes. He felt like he could sleep for a week, but he needed to work that day and he needed to figure out what he was supposed to do. Maybe he could Google it. Had Nic Cage ever bit anyone before? It seemed like something he would have heard about on Twitter.

Cameron was in the kitchen when he exited the bedroom. He and Cameron Sanderson had met in college and had been roommates for two years. Cameron ran his own graphic design business from the apartment and rarely went out. Most of his days were spent in his bedroom, but he did pop out to socialize with Stanley in the evenings and once or twice he even went out on dates or with friends, though it was more of a bi-monthly experience.

"Why does the apartment look like a murder scene?" he asked as Stanley entered the kitchen. He sat at the table eating a breakfast wrap with a Pepsi. Cameron ate like a man who didn't want to live to old age.

"Huh?" Stanley replied.

"The front door, the hallway, your door, the floor. Full on slasher movie blood trail."

"Oh. That was me," he answered.

"Did you kill someone?"

"No, I mean, it was my blood."

Cameron set his wrap down and took a sip of his drink.

"So, like, did you get murdered?"

Stanley sighed. He was going to sound insane, but if he couldn't trust Cameron, there was no one else for him to trust. His dad would have believed him, no questions asked. But he was gone. Stanley's mother had really pulled away after the divorce and it got worse after his dad died. He hadn't talked to her in over a year. She hadn't even remembered his last birthday.

For most of his life, Stanley had been alone. He'd had friends as a kid, but nothing that was long lasting. His family had moved around a lot, so he never had a chance to bond with many people. That's why he and his dad had been so close. That was also why Nic Cage became a sort of de facto hero.

His parents could move from state to state, and once even out of the country for a few years. But Nic Cage was reliable and consistent. He was always there, and he was always able to keep him and his dad entertained. That meant something. That was a real thing he could count on.

"Nic Cage bit me," he said bluntly. Cameron set his drink down.

"One more time?" he replied.

"Nic Cage bit me."

"Hmm," his roommate grunted. He moved his glass for no reason and slightly rotated his plate. "Go on."

"I went to that film festival last night, right?"

"Okay."

"And after it ended, I figured I could cut through the park on my way home."

"Okay."

"So I'm walking and I hear someone following me -"

"Nic Cage?" Cameron interrupted.

"No. Well, yes. But I didn't know that at the time. I thought it was a mugger or a stabber or something."

"Park's full of stabbers," Cameron agreed.

Stanley made a face and continued.

"Anyway, I started to run, and this guy runs after me. And then I think I lost him, but then he's in front of me and it's Nic Cage!"

"Famous actor Nic Cage?" Cameron clarified.

"Listen, I know how it sounds. But it was him. I talked to him for like five minutes. It was one hundred percent Nicolas Cage."

"And he bit you?"

"Okay, so we chatted for a minute and it was weird. I think he was just quoting his own movies at me. And then he grabbed my hand and pulled me against his body and bit me."

Cameron nodded his head and moved his glass again.

"That is literally the dumbest thing you have ever said."

"It's for real. Look!" Stanley said. He pulled his shirt up, groaning as he freed his arm. With his shirt half off, he leaned forward, showing the wound to his roommate.

"Dude," Cameron said, standing up to get a closer look. He leaned in, grimacing as he inspected it like a child looking at roadkill.

"Is it still oozing?" Stanley asked. He couldn't see it so well without a mirror.

"Yeah, it's oozing. That's a human bite, man."

"It was Nic Cage," he insisted again. Cameron looked up at him.

"You're serious?"

"Look at the damn thing! You can go check out the shirt I wore last night. It's covered in blood. Nic Cage bit me in the damn park."

"Huh."

Cameron looked at the wound again and then poked it unbidden. Stanley hissed, flinching away.

"Sorry," Cameron muttered. "Making sure it was real."

"Come on," Stanley said. His roommate shrugged.

"Alright. So Nicolas Cage bit you. Why?"

"If I knew that I'd... I don't know what I'd do. But I don't know, so it doesn't matter."

"Did he say anything? He wasn't all 'hey, can I taste you?' or whatever?"

"I think the last thing he said was 'papa's got a brand new bag.'"

Cameron laughed, then covered his mouth as though it had sneaked out.

"Oh my God, he didn't say that."

"He did."

Cameron laughed again, looking at the wound once more.

"This is so... you're sure it was Nic Cage?"

"Guy, it's me. No one knows Nic Cage as well as I do. I've been watching his movies most of my life. I have them all in my room."

"Yeah, I know. I mean... you weren't high, were you?"

"I don't smoke on work nights, you know that."

Cameron nodded and shrugged.

"Alright. So what now? Call the police?"

"I can't call the police. They'll think I'm insane."

"That's true," Cameron agreed. "Is Nic Cage even in town anymore? I thought they finished filming last week."

"They did. I can't make it make sense. I don't know why he chased me through the park and bit me. What kind of normal explanation for that is there?"

"Good point. But you need to do something about that. The ooze is yellow. You got yellow Cage ooze."

"I know. I heard a human mouth is dirtier than a dog's."

"Looks like Cage has a toilet mouth because that is a gnarly bite."

Stanley sighed. He'd majored in English in college and worked in a grocery store. Nothing in his life had prepared him for being attacked by a movie star in the park. This was uncharted territory.

"Do you have any ointment?" he asked then. Cameron took his seat once more and sipped his Pepsi.

"They don't make ointment for that. You need to go see a doctor."

"What doctor?"

"Dr. Strange, man, I don't know. Go to the clinic on Belmont. Tell them some girl you were making out with bit you. They'll give you some amoxicillin or something."

"A girl? What girl?" Stanley asked him. Cameron rolled his eyes.

"A made up girl who isn't Nic Cage. Tell them whatever you want. I'm just tossing out ideas."

Stanley walked to the front door and looked in the mirror on the wall by the coat rack. The bite was just as red and ugly as it had been in the bathroom. He really did need to see a doctor.

"You should call the cops when you're done," Cameron advised. "And a lawyer."

"A lawyer? What the hell for?" Stanley asked.

"To sue Nic Cage for biting you. This is how you get rich quick. You can be the Guy Who Got Bit By Nic Cage. That's cool."

"I don't want to sue Nic Cage," Stanley replied. He loved Nic Cage. As a fan, anyway. He couldn't get him in trouble. There had to be a reason why he did it. Maybe he was on medication. Or maybe it was heat stroke. He read somewhere that heat stroke was really dangerous.

"If you die from a Nic Cage bite, you're gonna feel stupid for not suing him."

"Maybe," Stanley agreed. He struggled back into his shirt and returned to his room to get his keys and phone before heading out. He had to give Nic Cage the benefit of the doubt. Why would the man bite a stranger in the park?

## Chapter Three

The Belmont Medical Walk-in Clinic was six blocks from Stanley's apartment and was located in a strip mall between an orthopedic shoe store and a shawarma restaurant. It routinely smelled delicious, which made the terrible wait times somewhat tolerable.

Normally, Stanley would avoid the clinic like the plague. He'd waited out severe diarrhea, a flu, and a sprained ankle without going to the clinic before, simply because he hated waiting there. He could have gone to the ER at the hospital but the wait there was inexplicably longer and once, when he was twelve, a man vomited on him in the hospital waiting room and he'd never been back since.

The waiting room was cramped with tiny seats like you'd find in a community center AA meeting. The kind with seventies-era upholstered seats that were designed for people who were as narrow as broomsticks. It forced you to choose to put a seat between you and the next person, which was all fine and good until too many people showed up, and then you had to touch the person next to you. The sick stranger next to you. The person who could have typhoid or leprosy. You didn't know. No one knew, that's why they were at a clinic.

Stanley tried to ignore the knowledge that the old lady in the seat next to him had a swollen, runny eye and was touching his leg as he stared at a TV on the wall. The waiting room TV was there not to entertain anyone, but as a refuge. It was a place to direct your eyes so you could at least avoid the trauma of eye contact. Everyone stared at it like it was a holy relic.

The TV was tuned to the local affiliate and ran down a list of what was going on in town over the weekend before returning to their top story. Stanley watched, his back rigid and his shoulder throbbing, as local anchor Hunter Grimsby informed viewers that police were investigating a murder in the park from the night before.

Details were scant, as they tend to be, and not even a name was released, but the reality of what was happening was not lost on Stanley. He had been attacked in the park. Someone had been murdered in the park. That meant there was a chance, however outlandish, that Nic Cage murdered someone.

Stanley wanted to leave. He felt anxiety building in him, and it twisted his guts like sriracha-fueled dysentery. He wanted to throw up and cry at the same time. But he couldn't leave. He couldn't even say anything. Because he didn't know anything for sure. He didn't know if Nic Cage killed a stranger. Just like he didn't know if Nic Cage had actually tried to murder him.

"Stanley Miller?" a voice asked. He looked around the room. The nurse from the desk was now standing at the door to the offices. She was taller than him and had long blonde hair. On another day he would have felt his stomach twisting not from Nic Cage murder fear but from mildly embarrassing awkwardness at realizing she was very pretty and was making eye contact with him.

"Hello," Stanley said. The nurse laughed, her expression somewhere between amused and confused.

"Hello. You can come back now," she said. Stanley felt foolish. Of course, that was why she'd called him. He stood up, avoiding the woman next to him, and walked over to her.

"Room two," she said, holding the door. The hallway beyond her was short and plain and had only three doors. He headed to the one marked two and opened it, stepping into a room with a small exam table ensconced in a paper shield and a desk that was adorned with jars of things like cotton swabs, disposable gloves, and a computer.

"Take a seat," the nurse said, gesturing to the exam table. It was just high enough to make it uncomfortable to sit on and he had to hop up to do so, making him feel oddly child-like.

"So what seems to be the problem today?" the nurse asked.

"Huh?" he replied. She raised her eyebrow at him. Her eyes were green and the left one had a small scar under it that added some charm and character to her face, which was already quite charming. Her crescent moon earrings reminded him of Lucky Charms. Stanley had not been on a date in two years.

"Why did you come here today, Mr. Miller?" she said.

"Stanley," he said. "You can call me. Call me Stanley, I mean," he told her.

"Okay, Stanley. Why are you here?"

"Yeah, okay. Nurse… Bruce?" he asked, reading the little nametag on the chest of her mint green scrubs. She frowned.

"Bruce is off today. He took my name tag. It's Nurse Wayland."

"Your name is Wayland?" Stanley asked.

"Sara Wayland, Stanley. And you are here because…?"

Stanley shifted nervously, making the paper sheet on the exam table crinkle loudly.

"Do you know Nic Cage?" he asked. Sara smiled at him.

"The actor? Not personally."

Stanley laughed.

"Oh, yeah. No. I mean, of course not. Okay, so last night there was a little Nic Cage film festival that I went to -"

"Hey, me too!" she said, her smile absolutely lighting up her face. Stanley found himself smiling back.

"For real?"

"Heck yeah. Like I'm not going to see *Face/Off* on a big screen with a hot dog and a liter of Sprite."

"That's awesome. Did you know they're showing *Vampire's Kiss* next weekend?"

"I did know that. But I'm not sure why that explains you being here."

"Right," Stanley said. The room was oddly cold, and there was a poster on the wall that showed a diagram of testicles. It was right over Sara's shoulder and his eyes kept drifting towards it.

"So after the movies I thought I'd walk home, and I went through the park."

"Okay…" Sara said.

"And I got bit."

There was a pause then. She fixed him with a curious stare, and it seemed like she was waiting for more.

"You got bit?" she asked.

"On the, uh, shoulder," he clarified. "Here."

He lifted his shirt and pulled one arm free, moving the fabric out of the way and exposing his shoulder. It felt hot to the touch, and it made him wince as the cotton of his t-shirt grated across it.

Sara came closer to him, grimacing very slightly despite trying to maintain her professionalism.

"That's a human bite," she said.

"Yeah," Stanley agreed.

"A person bit you. Who bit you?"

"It was an attack. In the park," he explained.

"You should have gone to the ER after it happened. It's quite inflamed."

"Yeah, I was just... I wanted to get home and get safe, you know?"

"So it was like a mugging? Did you call the police?" she asked him. He shook his head.

"Not a mugging."

"So someone just bit you for no reason? Who was it?"

Stanley's eyes drifted to the testicle poster. It was a cross section of the male anatomy and was speaking to the importance of self-examinations to help catch cancer early.

"Stanley?" Sara said.

"You're going to think I'm crazy," he said, lowering his voice very slightly.

"I assure you I won't," she told him.

Stanley took a deep breath. He didn't need to tell her. He didn't even need to tell the doctor. Who cared who bit him? A bite was a bite, right? But she was at the same theater. She was in the room with him. That had to mean something. That was kismet or serendipity. It was a sign.

"It was Nic Cage," he said in a voice that was barely more than a whisper, as though speaking his name louder might alert him to the fact he was being outed.

Nurse Sara stared at him with a totally unreadable expression on her face.

"Well, okay. The doctor will be in to see you shortly," she said, turning away from him and opening the door.

"I'm not crazy!" he said, louder than he wanted to.

"I didn't say anything," she replied.

"I know, and that's making me very anxious."

She closed the door almost all the way and then faced him once more.

"If you're worried I'm going to say anything, I won't. I'm a nurse. I hear unusual things all the time."

"I'm worried you don't believe me," he said then. Her eyes narrowed very slightly, as though she didn't understand what he was saying and was trying to figure it out.

"Why would it matter if I believe you?" she asked.

"It doesn't, I guess. But I still don't believe it myself because it doesn't make sense."

"So if I believe you, it makes it feel more real to you?"

"I don't know."

She stared at him for another awkwardly long moment. She looked confident and sure of herself and every moment of that made Stanley doubt what he'd experienced even more.

"Do you think it was actually Nic Cage who bit you?" she asked quietly. He shook his head without hesitation.

"No," he answered.

"Why?"

"I... it looked like him. It was him. It *was* him. He was quoting his own movies. But it couldn't be him because that's literally the dumbest thing I have ever heard of. So I don't know what really happened."

Sara smiled, and it was a coy and secretive smile that made her look mischievous and exciting. She reached for the doorknob again.

"You know what Socrates said about knowing and not knowing, right?"

"Not remotely," he answered honestly. He took an intro philosophy course in college, but it was at eight in the morning and he slept through most of it.

"Sometimes a smart man has to know that he doesn't know, Stanley."

"Oh."

She held the doorknob in her hand and gave him another considering glance.

"Can I tell you something?"

"Anything," he replied, regretting the obvious eagerness in his voice. She either didn't notice or didn't care.

"About a week ago, I met Nic Cage," she said. Stanley's eyes widened, but she continued before he could say anything. "He was in town for that movie, right? He was doing a stunt where he was supposed to kick Frank Grillo off a roof and he slipped on a loose shingle and fell on his ass, knocked his head on the roof. I had volunteered to work with medics on set just because I was hoping to maybe meet him, and I was the one who did the original assessment of his injury. Even patched up his bloody lip."

"Wow," Stanley said. "Isn't telling me that a violation of doctor patient privilege?"

"I'm not a doctor," she pointed out.

"Wow," he said again. "Did he bite you?"

Sara laughed and opened the door a little wider. He smiled and decided he liked her laugh very much. He had never met an attractive woman who was also a Nic Cage fan and also willing to talk to him. His last girlfriend had tolerated Cage movies but would also go on week-long color diets where she'd only eat white foods or purple foods and they never really meshed the way Stanley had hoped.

"The doctor will be in to see you in just a minute." She closed the door behind her.

Sara left and Stanley crinkled his paper seat, sitting with his shirt half on, staring at a testicle poster for twelve minutes.

When the doctor finally arrived, he had a distinct mustard stain on the lapel of his white coat. It was just one spot, a perfect yellow teardrop that was no doubt an escapee from a sandwich. The man himself looked to be about forty and he had a face that was so long it became a distraction from the words he was saying. He looked like Fred Gwynne if he was on a planet with too much face gravity.

"Mr. Miller?" the doctor said.

"What?" Stanley replied.

"It says you were bit. May I take a look?" he asked.

"Oh. Yes," he said, turning his shoulder towards the man.

"This is a human bite," the doctor pointed out. Stanley sighed.

"Yes."

"The human mouth has over six billion bacteria in it, did you know that?" He leaned in very close to inspect the bite and spoke into Stanley's shoulder. "People compare it to a toilet all the time, which isn't fair. We clean toilets with bleach and they're actually some of the cleanest things in a house, assuming proper housekeeping takes place. A human mouth is much dirtier."

"Oh, that's good to know," Stanley said. The doctor used the end of his pen to poke at the wound and Stanley winced.

"This was done last night?" he asked.

"Yeah. Some crazy person in the park."

The doctor lifted his head. He was inches from Stanley's face. He could smell the mustard on the man's breath now.

"Crazy is generally frowned upon as a term to describe those who may be suffering mental health issues, as the negative connotations can stigmatize people who may or may not be experiencing serious health concerns. Also, without a proper diagnosis of a mental health related issue, this is just speculation on your part and would be unfair at best and ableist at worst."

"Oh," Stanley stated. Sitting on the paper-covered table as he was, he had no way to back up to create space between himself and the doctor. "I just thought, since it was a stranger who bit me in the middle of the night, that there was something odd about him."

"Odd is a perfectly acceptable and appropriate term," the doctor agreed. "Getting bit by a stranger is odd. Did you notify police?"

"Not yet."

"You should," the doctor said. He leaned down again to inspect the wound once more.

"Your biter used a lot of force. It appears as though every tooth pierced your skin. That's not easy to do."

"Yeah. That's neat," Stanley said, unsure of how to respond.

"If you had come in right away, you could have had the wound cleaned with saline and properly dressed. As it is now, I can clean the outside a bit and prescribe you some antibiotics. You'll need to keep an eye on it and if the infection seems to be getting worse after a few days - more pain and inflammation, leaking pus, that sort of thing - you'll need to go to the hospital."

The doctor went to his desk and grabbed some supplies, then started in on cleaning the bite. Stanley stared at the testicles. It took him just a couple of minutes to clean it down and apply some ointment then a dressing. He wrote out a prescription on a pad of paper and then handed it to Stanley.

"Get that filled right away. I want you to take a double dose to start, then one pill three times daily until it's done, okay? Come back in ten days for a checkup unless it starts getting worse, then come in sooner."

"Okay," Stanley agreed, looking at the neatly written script. "You have nice penmanship."

"Everyone should practice their penmanship," the doctor said very seriously. "See you in ten days."

The doctor left the room while Stanley put his shirt back on. He slipped the prescription into his pocket and then headed back into the hallway. The doctor had vanished entirely. Stanley returned to the waiting room. There were about six new people there. The woman who had been sitting too close to him was gone. Sara was behind the desk at the front again.

"I have to come back in ten days," he told her.

"Well, I look forward to seeing you again," she said. He smiled and looked around the room to see if anyone else had been paying attention to her.

"Really?" he said. She laughed again.

"Take care of yourself, Stanley Miller. Avoid the park."

"Yeah," he agreed. He had no plans to ever visit the park again. "Anyway, goodbye."

He left the clinic and headed for home. His shift at work was starting in just over an hour, and he needed to get ready.

## Chapter Four

Cameron was gone by the time Stanley got back to the apartment. He got dressed for work quickly and headed back out again. Gates' Market was about fifteen minutes from his home and he liked to walk at a leisurely enough pace that he wasn't sweaty by the time he got there. One day he truly planned to buy a car, but he also planned to visit New Zealand and eat oysters and everything had to happen in its own time.

He stocked shelves at the market and his shoulder was still throbbing, but as long as he didn't get stuck in the back unloading pallets, he figured he'd be able to manage it. The work was mundane and repetitive, and that was actually why he enjoyed it. Clicking his brain off and still getting paid for it had a lot of appeal.

Work had been a major stressor in the lives of Stanley's parents. Always moving, always pushing, always trying to get a thing done. Work became their lives in many ways, and he always resented that. He'd seen it happen to friends and acquaintances as he grew older, so he realized it was not unique to just his family. People got lost in work. They became other people and worked themselves to death. His father did it literally.

Stanley got nothing out of work. He wanted money to live and so he did work that allowed that to happen. And when his shift was over, he couldn't have cared less about what he did or spare it a second thought. His work didn't matter, and that was something he took comfort in. How people managed to do the opposite was baffling to him.

Gil Henderson, Stanley's manager at Gates' Market, was not cut from the same cloth. In his world, Gates' Market may have very well been the only thing standing between humanity and utter chaos. The man acted like ensuring all the cans of beans on a shelf were facing the right direction was the most important task a person could undertake. Maybe ever. His seriousness had grown to legendary heights at the store, and during break periods, coworkers would often share tales of Gil's latest irrational rant.

Stanley did his best not to get on Gil's nerves because if he got on Gil's nerves Gil would get on his nerves and it became a terrible cycle of Gil talking to him and paying attention to his work, which Stanley hated.

Once, just after Stanley got the job, he left a dented can of corn on a shelf and Gil brought it up, daily, for three months. His thinking was that if Gates' Market didn't respect their customers enough to not show them dented corn, then the customers wouldn't respect them enough to shop there, the store would close, everyone would lose their jobs and be homeless. Stanley was making people homeless.

Gil was in the office and blissfully nowhere near Stanley, which meant his day was likely to be completely uneventful, which was how he wanted it. He filled shelves with new product, rotated out old product and repeated for eight entire hours with two fifteen minute breaks and a half hour lunch in the middle.

It was just after his second break while he was working in the condiment aisle when he realized that the music track playing over the store speakers had changed from the usual repetitive playlist he had heard a thousand times before.

The music was a mix of older Top Forty songs that had been vetted to be considered inoffensive background noise for shopping. They used to get a new mix every few months, but Gil had decided to save money by only updating the list once per year. Most customers would never notice because they only spent a limited time in the store. Stanley spent forty hours a week there. He knew Billy Joel's voice better than his own mother's.

The Spin Doctors were in the midst of explaining the story of Two Princes when Stanley stopped to listen.

*Marry him, your father will condone you*, the speakers crooned. *Sorry boss, but there's only two men I trust. One of them's me. The other's not you.*

"What?" Stanley said, holding a jar of mayonnaise. That was not a line from the song, he was sure of it.

*Marry him, marry me, I'm the one that loved you baby can't you see*, the song continued.

"Do you have these in a one gallon size?" a woman asked him suddenly, holding up a jar of relish.

"A gallon of relish?" he said, confused.

"Yes," the woman confirmed.

*We are here to ruin ourselves and to break our hearts and love the wrong people and die,* the Spin Doctors continued. That wasn't part of the song either.

"Is that *Moonstruck*?" Stanley asked.

"Is what *Moonstruck*?" the customer replied. He shook his head and looked at the relish.

"We don't have a gallon of relish. I don't think they make it by the gallon."

"I saw it in the internet," she assured him.

"In the internet?"

"Yes. It was in Amazon."

"I don't -" Stanley paused.

*I could eat a peach for hours*, the song continued. Stanley looked at the woman.

"Do you hear Nic Cage?" he asked her quietly.

"What? I just want relish," she told him. She was shorter than him and she was wearing a salmon colored dress. He could see the nape of her neck and thought, just for a moment, that maybe it would be a good idea to bite her to shut her up.

"Oh no," he whispered, covering his mouth with his hands.

"Are you on something?" the woman asked. Stanley shook his head, keeping his hands over his mouth.

*You and I share the same DNA. Is there anything more lonely than that?* The voice over the speakers was distinctly Nic Cage now, even though he was singing to the tune of Two Princes.

Stanley turned his back on the woman and walked quickly to the rear of the store, pushing through the doors into the storeroom. He stood alone next to a pallet of oatmeal and listened. The song finished as normal and a new song started. There was no Nic Cage. No lines from movies, no one emulating his voice. Everything was normal.

He considered for a moment that perhaps he was going crazy. Or he was mentally unwell. Was it offensive to call himself crazy? He didn't know. There were too many confusing things going on.

Stanley leaned against the pallet for a moment, just breathing and trying to stay calm. He closed his eyes and drifted back to the night before. It couldn't have been Nic Cage. How could it have been? It didn't make sense. It was probably a junkie who was so high his spit was hallucinogenic, and that made Stanley imagine it was Nic Cage because of the movies he'd just seen. That made sense, he was sure.

"Just a super high junkie," Stanley said, opening his eyes. He stared into the tiny face of Nic Cage on the label of a box of Quaker Oats. Nic Cage was the Quaker Oats man.

Stanley screamed and stumbled back, falling down against a case of rice. Uncle Ben had been replaced with Nic Cage as well, his grinning face hovering above some teriyaki style rice with peas and carrots.

He scrambled backward on all fours, turning away from the packages and focusing on the cement floor. The junkie must have been very high. Too high. Stanley didn't know a lot about drugs, but he knew mushrooms did that sort of thing to people. Maybe he walked through some on his way home, some dangerous wild mushrooms and now he was head to toe infected. He needed to work it through his system.

"Stanley?" someone asked. He turned his head and saw Dolores, one of the cashiers, in the back on her break.

"Yes?" he replied.

"Are you alright?"

"I'm well. I'm just using the restroom."

He scrambled towards the bathroom on all fours, then stood up at the door.

"Thank you for your concern," he said to Dolores, slipping inside and closing the door.

The employee bathroom was small and smelled of orange cleanser mixed with urine. There was a toilet, a sink with a rusty drain, and a plunger that no one ever wanted to touch. Stanley looked at himself in the mirror over the sink.

He was pale, and sweat beaded around his hairline. He was breathing as though he'd just been running, and he realized he needed to calm down. He was working himself up, and that had to be making things worse.

The tap squeaked as he turned on the cold water and he cupped his hands under it, splashing it on his face. The cold was a shock to his system, but he enjoyed it. It was good. He felt more focused and in control right away.

Stanley had never had a panic attack before, but he thought that might have been what was happening. Just a Nic Cage-induced panic attack. People probably had those all the time.

Another splash of cold water sent a chill through him that was oddly relaxing. He turned off the tap and then unlocked the door. Dolores was still standing outside of the break room.

"Did you need to use the facilities?" Stanley asked. She shook her head. "Very well. Please enjoy the rest of your break." He headed back into the store as nonchalantly as he could. He didn't want to weird anyone out more than he already had. That included himself.

The relish lady was gone. Stanley stood next to the mayonnaise and took one last, calming breath. He started working again, trying to stay focused and on task. A song by Prince came on and he didn't slip into Nic Cage monologing once. Things were back on track.

Stanley loaded jars on the shelf. His shoulder throbbed with each one. Just a twinge, a little bit of heat, enough to make sure he wasn't going to forget what happened any time soon.

"Excuse me, do you know where the mayo is?" a man with graying hair and round, wire-rimmed glasses asked. Stanley looked at the mayo in his hand and then at the man.

"Why am I a drunk? Is that really what you wanna ask me?" Stanley said to the man. He dropped the mayo on the floor and covered his mouth again. The jar shattered.

"What the hell?" the man said.

"Look at me," Stanley said between his fingers. "I'm a prickly pear."

He gasped and clamped his hand harder over his mouth. Those were lines from *Leaving Las Vegas*. He was quoting Nic Cage. He wasn't trying to. He didn't want to.

"What the hell are you doing?" the man asked. He had mayo splattered on his shoes.

"I'm…" Stanley started, trying to force the answer he was thinking and not something from a random Nic Cage movie. "I'm going to steal the Declaration of Independence."

In his head, Stanley cursed. The man said something else to him, but he didn't hear it. Instead, he headed towards the front of the store. He made his way to Gil's office, despite not wanting to do so, and knocked on the door.

"Come," Gil called. Stanley opened the door.

"I feel like my skull is on fire," Stanley blurted out. Gil looked up from his desk. He often pretended to be doing work, but everyone knew he played Solitaire for at least two hours a day. He probably would have played different games, but the man still didn't know how to use the internet.

"You're sick?" Gil said.

"I'm having a hard time concentrating," he replied. He vaguely recalled the line from the movie *The Rock*, but he was at least trying to give relevant answers.

"Are you serious right now, Stanley? Your shift is almost over. You can't finish it out?"

"I knock things over and I throw up all the time," he said. Gil looked offended and Dolores appeared behind Stanley suddenly.

"Someone dropped a jar of mayo in aisle four. Was that you?" she said to Stanley. He nodded, looking from her to Gil. Gil sighed loudly and dramatically.

"Good grief. Clock out. Go see a doctor or something. Next time, call in before your shift if you're going to be stumbling around here sick."

He wanted to say something more, but feared what might come out of his mouth. Instead, he gave Gil an enthusiastic thumbs up and turned away, leaving as quickly as he could.

## Chapter Five

Stanley walked home at a forced leisurely pace. He stopped at his drugstore and filled his prescription, then bought himself some microwave popcorn. The day was dragging on and the sun was already beginning to set. The sky was filled with flashes of colors from pink to orange to purple, and the full moon had already risen.

Stanley stopped on the sidewalk, his eyes locked on the moon. He couldn't recall ever seeing it so large and so clear in the sky. It looked like a scene from a film.

The definition was as clear as it was in photographs from NASA. He could make out the craters and terrain, all cast in white. It was breathtaking.

Stanley blinked. The moon was silver, and the sky was black. He looked around in confusion. Cars drove down the street and people walked past him, ignoring him the way everyone ignored everyone else on a sidewalk. He looked at his watch. He had left work over two hours earlier. He'd been staring at the moon for more than half that time.

He felt his stomach twist and growl. His shoulder was itchy and achy. He needed to get home.

Head down, Stanley trudged on. He felt the urge to stare up again, but resisted. His face was hot and his hair felt like it was moving. He ran a hand through it, but it seemed fine. There was no motion. Nothing was crawling through it, either.

He made it back to the apartment feeling flushed and lightheaded. His skin felt like it was burning.

"Stan, that you?" Cameron shouted from his room.

"Killing me won't bring back your goddamn honey!" Stanley shouted back.

"Okay, good to know," his roommate replied.

Stanley rushed to his room and closed the door. He headed to the bathroom, peeling his t-shirt off and looking at himself in the mirror again.

His skin was flush and dewy with sweat. He turned on the tap and popped two of the antibiotics into his mouth, using his hand to slurp up water and swallow them. He turned on the shower and stripped off the rest of his clothes before getting in and letting the cold water cascade over his body.

When he was finished, he returned to his room. His head was still swimming, and it reminded him of the first time he'd gotten drunk at a party in high school. He had no idea how much vodka was too much vodka and they were raiding his friend Tommy's liquor cabinet, so no one really cared, either. He remembered feeling light and airy until he threw up on Tommy's sofa.

Stanley stood in his bedroom. Moonlight flooded in from the break in his curtains. His hands were tingling, faint prickles, like the sensation of having slept on his arm and cut off the circulation.

A noise from his stomach preceded a sharp cramp that made him double over. His guts churned like he had spent the day eating room temperature shrimp salad. The numbness in his hands spread up his arms. His legs felt like jelly, and he collapsed to his hands and knees.

"Please," he whispered, though he had no idea who he might be talking to. His teeth felt strange in his mouth. Like they had changed shape or grown larger. Something was very wrong.

Stanley tried to get to his feet and failed. His stomach lurched, and he felt acid slide up his throat to the back of his tongue. He tasted sour metal and fire. The muscles of his arms quivered. Pressure built in his head, slowly at first, but then faster. He felt like something was trying to push his eyes out from the inside.

Something popped in his back, deep in the muscle. His ribs felt like they were trying to pull apart and he tried to scream, but no sound came out. The flesh on his hands moved before his eyes, rolling like a tarp covering a pile of snakes.

He could hear his own hair rustling as his skull snapped inside his head like a cracker. It spread and expanded, stretching the flesh of his face. The pain was immense, but no scream would come from his mouth. He felt like something was choking him, like a rag had been stuffed deep in his throat.

Stanley collapsed in a heap. His skin continued to crawl and his kneecaps popped and shifted in his legs. His jaw snapped, and the pain caused him to lose his vision before it slowly returned in a series of flashes of lights and colors. His entire body was being rearranged from the inside out.

Muffled gurgles escaped his throat. He tasted blood and fire. Bones moved in his pelvis and he vomited onto his bedroom floor, finally getting the tail end of a scream from his lips. And just like that, it was all over.

Stanley sat up. The pain was gone. All of it was gone, even from the bite in his shoulder. But he felt different. He felt thicker, somehow. He looked at his own hands and frowned. They were not his own hands at all. The flesh was lined and older looking. They were too hairy. They looked rough and strange and wrong.

He got to his feet and stumbled to the bathroom. His legs weren't working properly. Not that they didn't work, they didn't work right. Because they weren't his legs.

A faint gasp escaped his lips as he turned the bathroom light on. He had almost been expecting what he was seeing and yet, confirming it for real, it was still hard to believe. Impossible to believe.

Stanley touched his own face, and watched in the mirror as he did not touch his own face at all. He watched Nicolas Cage touching his own face. Nicolas Cage's hands doing what Stanley felt he was doing with his own hands. He leaned forward and watched Nic Cage lean forward. He opened his mouth and watched Nic Cage open his mouth.

"I'm Nic Cage," he said. His hairline had receded. His eyes had grown wider. They were brown normally, but now they were blue. Everything was different. Everything was completely Nic Cage.

He looked down at his own body. He was naked Nic Cage from head to toe.

"Oh my God," he muttered. The urge to quote a movie bubbled up in his head, but he pushed it down again. Adrenaline ran through his veins and he could feel his muscles almost vibrate from it.

His breath came in gasps as he stared into eyes that were not his own. He closed them, shutting out the image of Cage and just stood still in his bathroom, breathing quickly and trying to calm himself down. There had to be an explanation for what was happening. He just needed to think rationally. He needed to get a grip on things and calm down and be smart.

He opened his eyes again. Nic Cage's worried face stared back at him. He shook his head and looked down, turning the water on. He let it run over his hands, cold and clean. The skin didn't change, though. The hands wouldn't wash away.

Stanley reluctantly looked at himself again. Looked at Nic Cage's face. He shook his head and held his breath. He tried to push, though he wasn't sure what he was pushing. Pushing his mind, and his internal organs. He was trying to push himself back into himself. He needed to push Nic Cage out. He didn't belong there.

He grunted and even that sounded husky and foreign in his mouth. It was a solid Nic Cage grunt, not a familiar Stanley Miller grunt. Nothing was changing. He was not uncagefying himself.

The wound on his shoulder had faded but not vanished, and he could still feel it throbbing.

"Hey Stan, you hungry?" Cameron asked from out in the apartment.

"Uh, I'm fine. Everything's fine."

"What happened to your voice?" came Cameron's muffled reply.

Stanley frowned at himself in the mirror. He sounded like Nic Cage.

"Nothing. You think fish have dreams?" he asked, then cursed quietly and covered his mouth. He had to concentrate on what he wanted to say, or it seemed like a random Cage quote would roll out.

"I dunno, buddy. Has that been a concern of yours for a while?" Cameron called back. Stanley simply grunted, hoping that would suffice.

Things were weird and getting weirder, and Stanley was not a fan. He was also left with the stark realization that what had happened to him was all too real. Nicolas Cage stalked him through a park and bit him after spouting off random movie quotes. It made sense now. Not in a logical way, but in a way that put some pieces of a puzzle together.

Stanley walked back into his bedroom, then headed to the window. He threw open the curtains. Moonlight splashed across his face and he could feel something stirring in his chest. A desire to leap from the window, to hit the streets at a dead run and to just tear through the night like a wild animal.

He turned away from the window and took a shuddering breath. How could something not make any sense yet seem so obvious at the same time? He was bitten by Nic Cage and that bite turned him into Nic Cage. That was what happened. That was a thing. He was a lycagethrope.

The person who had bitten him was still out there. They looked like Nic Cage, but he knew now it wasn't the man himself. Just someone wearing his face. But why they bit him was still a mystery. As was who bit them. Did this go back to Nic Cage being in town? That was too much of a coincidence. There was something he wasn't seeing, though, and he needed to know more.

Stanley got dressed quickly, his clothes fitting oddly over a body that wasn't really his. He left his phone and keys at home and opened the window to crawl out onto the fire escape.

The air smelled crisp and alive. It smelled like coconut sunscreen and cigar smoke. It smelled like a fresh bottle of Pepsi and garlic bread. It was delicious and unlike anything he had ever experienced before.

Stanley looked out over the street. He could hear the car engines humming and buzzing along as they passed by. He caught snippets of conversations drifting from open windows. It was as though he had never been outside before in his life until just that moment.

Despite himself, despite the fear and uncertainty and the sense of panic that had gripped him like grim death only moments earlier, Stanley laughed. He had never felt anything like it ever before. Being in the world as Nic Cage was almost indescribable.

As a boy, Stanley would watch those Nic Cage movies and see himself in them. They were an escape. And it wasn't that his life was miserable. His parents were never abusive. He wasn't living in poverty. In a lot of ways, he had a very blessed upbringing. But in a lot of other ways, things were lacking as well.

After he lost his father, his mother had worked her fingers to the bone. They were already divorced, but the effect was profound. She and Stanley grew even further apart because of that and never really came together again. He had no other connections to fall back on. Moving around ensured that there were no friends, no support systems out in the world. So Stanley retreated into himself. He watched movies; he read comic books; he did his best to get through school and become an adult and do what adults do. He got a job stocking shelves. He lived day to day.

It was hard sometimes to remember what his dreams were. Every kid had dreams. But those astronaut and firefighter dreams belonged to someone else, it seemed. His life had turned into a three-part tragedy. The happy family, the broken family, and then after his father's death.

The thing was, that was Stanley's life. And standing on that fire escape, breathing the rich night air like he had never breathed it in before, he was not Stanley Miller. He was Nicolas Cage, movie star.

He wondered if that was truly how Nic Cage felt. Did he see and smell and hear the world the way Stanley was now hearing it? What an amazing way to live.

Stanley climbed down the fire escape ladder to the alley next to his apartment building. He still needed to find Nic Cage, the one that had bitten him. He needed to know what was happening and why. Most of all, he needed to know how to fix it.

He hit the alley and adjusted his ill-fitting clothes. He could smell the dampness, but it wasn't stale and mildewy like it usually was. It was like peat moss and old leather. Every breath Nic Cage took was an olfactory adventure.

The information Stanley had available was remarkably limited. He was bitten by Nic Cage in the park. And that was it. That was all he had to go on. So that would be the plan. He needed to find Bitey Cage and get answers.

He drifted out into the night, trying to keep his head down and not look at anyone either walking or driving. At first, it was just a result of his own discomfort in his new body. His strides were awkward and ill-timed because his legs weren't the same length that they had been that morning. But he soon realized if people were seeing Nic Cage walk down the street, that would draw a lot of unwanted attention. He didn't need that, not when he was looking for a second Cage in the night.

Stanley stuck to the shadows as much as possible as he made his way back to the park. It was much earlier than it had been when he was attacked and there were more people out and about, making him both nervous and paranoid. He glanced quickly at faces as he made his way into the park, trying to shield his own so no one would recognize him.

The urge to belt out quotes from Nic Cage movies bubbled up every time he saw another person. They came to mind unbidden, and sometimes he didn't even recognize the films they had come from.

He left the paths and stuck to the wooded areas of the park, drifting through the shadows and keeping his distance from people on walks or just cutting from one side of the park to the other. Though it was dark, most businesses in the area were still open and foot traffic was as busy as it was likely to get. Finding Bitey Cage would be harder than he had thought. Of course, he hadn't really thought. He was being reactionary and panicky. He hadn't thought anything through, and that was becoming very clear.

Stanley wandered the park from south to north, then east to west. It was a large green space, the biggest in town, and offered a lot of walking paths, hiking trails and places to picnic or play or whatever it was that people liked to do in parks. It offered a lot of places to hide.

By the western entrance, he found himself creeping along through the treeline as he heard voices and caught lights up ahead. He'd been out for over an hour and as the night wore on, fewer and fewer people were making use of the park. He was hoping that would increase his chances of finding Bitey Cage.

As he grew closer to the sounds near the entrance, a beam of light hit him square in the face, blinding him. He cursed and covered his eyes with his hands.

"Something bad is about to happen. I can feel it," he muttered, stumbling back.

"Keep your hands where I can see them," someone shouted in a stern tone.

"What?" Stanley asked, looking through his spread fingers. The flashlight beam was still right in his face and he couldn't see who was holding it, but he could tell there were at least two of them.

"Hands up and walk towards me slowly," another voice demanded. Stanley squinted, and the light wavered very slightly. He could see a police officer with a gun trained on him standing a short distance from the one holding the flashlight.

"I'm just out here walking -"

"Then you don't need to be talking right now. Step out onto the path here and then we can get to know each other, yeah?" the first voice said.

Stanley cursed again in his own head and took a tentative step forward. This was the last thing he wanted to do, but he wasn't going to try to run from the police, either. He'd never been especially good at talking his way out of anything, nor was he good at dealing with guns pointed at him. He was just learning for the first time.

"Why you lurking about in the trees?" one of the officers asked.

"Just walking," Stanley said, getting out of the trees onto the paved path.

"So you said," the second officer replied. "Tell me your name."

The officer with his gun drawn approached Stanley while the other kept his light on him.

"Stanley," he replied.

"Stanley what?"

"Stanley Miller," he said as the officer closed the gap between them.

"Okay, Stanley, put your hands down."

Stanley hesitated and then lowered his hands. He smiled and tried to look casual. The officer in front of him looked like he was maybe ten years older than Stanley, with a buzzed haircut and a visible neck tattoo creeping out from under his collar. He raised an eyebrow and stared Stanley in the eye.

"Nicolas Cage?" he said. The flashlight beam bobbed and the other officer came closer.

"Get the hell out," he said.

"Hey," Stanley said, trying to look and sound as cool as possible.

"Oh wow, Mr. Cage, it's great to meet you," the flashlight officer said, lowering the beam and approaching. He was younger and thinner than the first officer, and had curly, red hair atop his head.

The officer held out his hand and Stanley took it, unsure but willing to roll with it. They shook hands vigorously.

"I thought you guys packed up shop a week ago," the tattooed officer said. Stanley half shrugged.

"I'm just finishing up some stuff," he replied.

"You have got to be careful, Mr. Cage," the officer said, holstering his weapon. "Did you know there was a murder in this park last night?"

"Oh," Stanley answered. He had seen that on the news and was aware. But would Nic Cage be aware? Probably not.

"We've actually been asking people to stay out of the park tonight while we continue our investigation."

"Makes sense," Stanley agreed.

"Would it be cool if I got a selfie?" the red-haired officer asked.

"Walsh!" The tattooed officer sounded annoyed and his partner shrugged.

"No, sure. That's cool," Stanley said. Walsh grinned and pulled out his cell phone, handing it to the other man.

"You mind?" Walsh asked. His partner scoffed and held the phone up. Walsh put his arm around Stanley and leaned close to him. Stanley smiled at the other officer and the flash went off.

"Oh man, that's awesome. Thank you," Walsh said, shaking Stanley's hand again.

"Yeah, sure. Love the boys in blue!" Stanley stated, realizing how dumb it sounded the moment the words crossed his lips.

"Awesome," Walsh said, as though Stanley had just said something profound.

"If we're done," the tattooed cop said to his partner. Walsh nodded and put his phone away. "Mr. Cage, you're going to want to head back to wherever you're staying, or at least stay out of the park for now."

"Oh yeah, definitely. Dangerous times," Stanley agreed. "What, uh, happened? Can I ask that?"

"It was something," Walsh said. "Guy walking his dog was partially eaten. Can you believe that?"

"Walsh!" the other officer barked. Walsh shrugged.

"It's Nic Cage. Who's he going to tell?"

"Oh, no one," Stanley assured them. "Mum's the word."

"Mom?" Walsh asked.

"Just an expression," Stanley replied. "So no idea who attacked the guy, huh? Like who I should look out for or anything like that?"

"No witnesses, unfortunately," the tattooed officer told him. "But we've boosted patrols and are recommending people such as yourself try to avoid the park after dark while we investigate."

"No, yeah, sure. Great advice. Good, uh, policing," Stanley said, trying to say what he thought Nic Cage would say. He turned around and scanned the night.

"Should I head back the way I came or -"

A wordless scream interrupted Stanley as someone ran from the darkness at the three men. A blur of shadow on shadow was all he saw before Walsh was rocked backward onto the path.

The tattooed officer had his gun drawn before Stanley even realized what was happening. Walsh hit the ground with a surprised shout that turned into a grunt and then screamed as the dark figure that had tackled him began beating him.

"Back away now or I'll shoot!" the tattooed officer demanded, his gun trained on the dark figure. "I'm not warning you again!"

The figure snarled and lifted its head. Light from the streets hit the face and Stanley felt his stomach knot. Though there was blood on the man's lips, the face was unmistakable. It was Nic Cage.

"What the hell is this?" the officer said, looking from the man on top of Walsh to Stanley and back.

The raging Cage bared his teeth.

"How'd it get burned?" he demanded, spitting blood as he did so. The tattooed officer took a single step, and Cage lunged forward. The gun sounded like an explosion and Stanley flinched. He couldn't see where the bullet hit the man, but he fell back in a heap on top of Walsh.

"What the hell is going on?" the officer yelled, turning the gun on Stanley. Stanley put his hands up and shook his head.

"It's not me! I'm not… I don't even know," he said, stumbling over his words.

Something else rustled in the trees and a low, strange growl preceded a new shape's appearance. The officer fired again but missed as the new figure was smaller and lower to the ground.

Stanley opened his mouth, but no words came out as he watched a small, naked Nicolas Cage leap from the ground onto the officer, shaking his head furiously as his teeth clamped on the man's neck.

Both officer and small Cage fell to the ground. Little Cage growled and chuffed and tore at the officer's throat so violently a spray of blood splashed back and hit Stanley in the face.

"Oh my God…" Stanley muttered. The small Cage on the man's chest lifted its head and looked back. It was Nic Cage, there was no doubt, but aside from being nude, he wore a thick, black collar around his neck with a braided leash hanging from it. He looked to be no more than two feet tall, probably less.

Stanley gasped, and the small Cage growled, bearing bloody teeth. He looked from the savage little monster to the man collapsed on top of Walsh. A man walking his dog was what the police had told him. A man. And his dog.

Stanley looked back at the Cage on the leash. The dog had been bitten. And then, just like Stanley, it turned into Nic Cage under the full moon. He was looking at a dog Cage.

"Good boy," Stanley said, taking a tentative step back. Dog Cage's bloody lip curled, and he stomped his little feet on the officer's chest. At the same time, Raging Cage let out a loud exhale, as though he had just surfaced after swimming. He pushed himself up shakily from on top of the fallen officer and shook his head.

Dog Cage yipped and Raging Cage turned his head, looking at the smaller version of himself.

"I'm one of those fortunate people who like my job, sir," he said, getting shakily to his feet. Wherever the officer had shot him, it hadn't seemed to work well. Dog Cage made a questionable sound and cocked his head to one side.

Stanley took another step back and Raging Cage turned on him immediately. The manic smile of Nic Cage spread across his bloody lips and he rushed forward. Stanley winced, expecting to join the dead officer, and squeezed his eyes shut tightly. He was going to die as Nic Cage in a park, having accomplished literally nothing at all with his life. No one would even know what happened to him. They'd just find Nic Cage's half eaten corpse. It'd probably be on TMZ.

He could feel the warmth of the other man's body as his face was thrust into Stanley's. The other Cage breathed deeply and then began snorting. Stanley tentatively opened one eye and watched as Raging Cage snuffled and snorted around Stanley's neck and chest like an animal.

Dog Cage joined his master, smelling Stanley's shins down to his shoes. They circled him as he stood frozen, his entire body tense and awkward, until finally Raging Cage came back around to look him in the eye.

"Well, Baby-O, it's not exactly mai tais and Yahtzee out here," he said. Stanley raised an eyebrow. Raging Cage was breathing heavily, his face just inches from Stanley's own.

"Right," Stanley answered. "Uh… I just stole fifty cars in one night," he added, quoting *Gone in Sixty Seconds*.

Raging Cage gnashed his teeth and turned away quickly. He ran, half hunched over, back into the park. Dog Cage growled and exhaled loudly, blowing blood and spit across Stanley's shoe, and then ran after the other. Stanley was left alone with the corpses of two police officers and the distant sound of sirens growing closer.

He approached the fallen officers slowly. The man with the tattoos' eyes were still open, a massive chunk of his throat torn free. Even in the dim light, Stanley could see the glistening blood pooling under him.

Walsh had suffered the same fate. Raging Cage had bit his throat open only much more brutally than the smaller Cage, nearly taking the man's head completely off. He had seemed like a really nice guy and now he was just a bloody mess on a path in the park.

The only dead body Stanley had ever seen before was his father's. Stanley had been in his own apartment for just four months and he was heading back to his father's place to just hang out. They had agreed that Stanley would come home when he could so they could keep up with their tradition of watching movies and having dinner and just catching up on what was going on in each other's lives.

Part of the reason he was heading home that day was to see how his dad was feeling. He knew his dad was sick, but that was as deep as it got. No name on it. Certainly not cancer. He just hadn't been feeling well. But he assured Stanley he was fine, that he'd gone to the doctor and they took some blood and everything was going to be fine.

Instead, Stanley let himself in and found his father on the sofa. There was a half empty glass of soda on the table next to him and a bowl of plain potato chips. He'd been watching a cooking show on the Food Network.

Stanley found out later that his father had been diagnosed already and had been given only a few months to live. But it had become far more aggressive than the doctors had predicted and he had run out of time before he had even had a chance to tell anyone.

He had no idea if his dad planned to tell him ever or not. Maybe he went the way he wanted. Maybe he was going to tell Stanley that very day. He had no idea. Instead, he just found his father's room temperature body, and they never got to speak again.

The police officers looked nothing like his father had. They had been torn apart as though by animals. His father looked like he had fallen asleep. Seeing how things could have been, how some people had to meet their end, he was glad for whatever brief mercy might have been visited on his father.

Dying suddenly, in the middle of a snack on your own sofa, had to be one of the better ways to go. No pain and no fear. No Nic Cage ripping your throat out.

The sirens were drawing closer. The answers Stanley was hoping for would not be found if he was arrested for killing two police officers. He needed to run.

Stanley bolted into the night, running back into the park through the shadows in the direction from which he'd come. Part of him wanted to chase after Raging Cage and Dog Cage, but he feared both of them and wanted to keep as far away as he could. They were not the ones that had bitten him. He didn't know exactly how he knew that Raging Cage was not the one that had bitten him, but he did. There was simply something different about him.

The fact that there was a small Nic Cage on a leash made it seem clear to Stanley that both the man and his dog who were supposed to have been killed the night before had not died at all, but had been turned into Nic Cages themselves. But there was something wrong with them. They were feral and savage. There was nothing about being Nic Cage that made Stanley want to tear out throats. It didn't make sense. But neither did anything else.

Stanley wanted to find Bitey Cage, the one that had made him the way he was. But there was no way that was the source. No one just became Nic Cage, did they? There had to be a source. The Alpha Cage. That was who Stanley needed to find. But with the others in the park and the police on the way, he had no chance of investigating on his own. And if anyone had seen what had just happened, then all the police in town would soon be looking to arrest Nic Cage for murder. Things were getting out of hand faster and faster.

He ran through the shadows towards the far side of the park. When he saw an opening with no one around, he ducked back onto the street, keeping his head down.

## Chapter Six

It was not so late yet that no one was around on the streets and Stanley felt panic every time a car drove past. He glanced up each time, fearful that the police were about to roll up on him just as the officers unloaded their weapons into his face.

There were no police that he could see, but the sounds of sirens from the far side of the park made their way to his ears. He couldn't tell if they had found Walsh and his partner yet, but if they hadn't, they would soon.

He walked as casually as he could. He was not a man running from the police; he was just a guy out for a walk. Just another pedestrian no one needed to make eye contact with, slightly splattered in blood.

His mind was racing as much as his heart and he didn't think about where his feet were taking him. When he finally looked up, he found himself outside the movie theater once more. He was face to face with his own face, or rather Nic Cage's face, on a poster for the movie *Mandy*. Mandy Cage was bearded and more grizzled. Stanley Cage was smooth shaven but looking tired and manic. He looked like he needed a good nap and maybe a stiff drink. He felt the same way.

Trying to stay out of sight in front of a poster of the man whose body he was in was a stupid plan. He turned away from the theater and headed further downtown. He needed to kill time, and he needed to clear his head. He was a college graduate, there was a way out of this for sure.

A bite had turned him into Nic Cage. Of that, he was fairly certain. But the other Nic Cage's he had met were not like him. Bitey Cage only spoke in Cage quotes. Raging Cage was like an animal, and Dog Cage literally was an animal. What was the difference between them all?

The police said the man and his dog had been killed. Maybe they had been. Werewolves only died when they got shot by silver, as far as Stanley knew. So maybe a wereCage was the same. But Stanley had only gotten a single bite, so maybe he was less Cage than the others. Maybe it was the difference between taking a bit of undercooked chicken and eating an entire bucket of it.

"How many maybes is that?" Stanley said to himself as he walked. He glanced around to make sure no one heard him and saw that he was alone and only a few doors down from the local comic book shop. His feet seemed to be plotting their own path through town, further and further from his own home and from the park.

The night air was growing cold and his heart had slowed down to something closer to a human rate. He wanted to go home and get Cameron to help him, but there was no real help Cameron could offer. He wanted to head back to the clinic and tell nurse Sara that he was in need of medical help and then maybe ask her on a date. If he was hiding inside of Nic Cage, it wouldn't be awkward or hard to do. He wanted a hundred and one things, none of which would really help with the problem at hand.

His feet set a course independent of his own thoughts. He knew he needed to keep moving, and that was what he did. Move and try to think of a plan. But that was all his head was allowing him to do - think about thinking about it. There was no real plan being born.

The fact was, Stanley had never been a man of action. Decisive thought, grand schemes. Who the hell did that sort of thing? That was movie stuff. Nic Cage stuff.

As a child, his father made all the big decisions and his mother went along with it. He realized later in life that it was less "going along" and more not being given a choice. His father wasn't perfect, not by any means. But things seemed good at the time. Things always seem good at the time.

When his father had died and Stanley was barely speaking to his mother, he had to become a real person. He had to make all the decisions and live like a real man. When the sink clogged, he had to figure out how to get inside the drain and pull out the greasy sludge. When the cable company overcharged him, he had to spend three hours on hold with customer service.

The things he did were not triumphs. They were not heroic or world changing. They were the little successes that a million people do a million times every day. But they were his little successes. They were him taking control of a world over which he'd had no control before.

No one prepares you for being your own person. Not really. Or maybe they do. Stanley didn't know. Maybe all the other kids in the world were being told how to do their taxes and shop for blenders and cook chicken to the right temperature. But Stanley hadn't really learned much of that, so he took each challenge as it came and did his best with it.

It was kind of shameful when he thought about it. How proud he had been of doing such simple, unimportant things. How much they made him think like he was really making it as an independent man. What an idiot he was.

He had just watched two police officers get murdered before his eyes. And he had every reason to believe they weren't truly dead. They could return as more Nic Cages. There could have been a slowly growing army of them, feral and bloodthirsty, stalking the night and killing whomever they discovered. If that was the case, Stanley might have been the only person who knew what was going on. He might have been the only person who could stop it.

In his mind, this was that moment. That Eminem "one shot" moment. The "step up to the plate" thing that people on TV talked about. But Stanley didn't know what stepping up to the plate even meant. Where was the damn plate and what happened when you finished stepping? No one ever said that.

Dad had never told Stanley what to do if a celebrity bites him in the park and then eats the throat out of two police officers. He'd not seen a how-to video on the subject on YouTube, either. He had nowhere to start.

The most frustrating part of dealing with what had happened was that Stanley could feel what had happened to him pulling him down. He felt like his mind was stuck in the mud and slowly sinking. Only in this case it wasn't just darkness waiting for him, it was Nic Cage.

The words still bubbled up unbidden in his mind. Quotes from movies, famous lines that he could not just hear but feel in his own head. He wanted to yell them, to act them out just as Cage had on screen. He wanted to sink his teeth into the world itself and make it take notice of him. And it terrified him.

He stopped walking. Before him, a massive set of stone stairs led up to a large, familiar building. He had come to the natural history museum. He hadn't been there in years, but it was the most easily identifiable building in town. Why had he walked there?

In the dark, the stone columns out front of the museum looked ominous and unwelcoming, though as a kid he'd always thought such things were sort of regal. They reminded him of Greek history.

He walked up the steps to the door of the museum, and the overwhelming urge to just break them down overcame him. He laughed, because of course he'd never do that. He kept laughing even as he put his foot through the glass door, shattering it into a million pieces.

The alarm went off and his laughter came forth in uncontrollable bursts. In the lobby of the museum was a dinosaur display. He sprinted across the glass and grabbed the skull of a Utahraptor and yanked it off of the reconstructed skeleton. He tucked it under his arm like a football, albeit a large and awkward one, and ran back out the destroyed door.

Somewhere in the back of his mind, he knew what he was doing was wrong. It wasn't even him. But the feeling was not only overwhelming, it was exciting. It felt like he was really living. He was Nic Cage. A crazed, baffling Nic Cage. The best Nic Cage and he loved it.

Sirens filled the night. Sirens approaching the museum, and sirens in the distance near the park. Stanley ran with his purloined dinosaur skull and just let his feet carry him. With each step, he drifted further and further into himself. He was letting Nic Cage take the wheel, and he was okay with it. It was liberating.

His anxiety was just washing away. His stress and worries, new and old, didn't seem to matter at all anymore. His father, dead police officers. What did any of it matter? He was wind sprinting through the night with a stolen fossil. It felt great.

The sirens faded into oblivion. Stanley faded into oblivion.

***

Sunlight slapped Stanley awake, and he grimaced, shielding his eyes. A breeze was rustling his nether regions, and it occurred to him even before he could see his surroundings he was naked and outside, two things he traditionally did not like to combine.

He sat up quickly and looked around. He was between two Ford Mustangs in a cement parking lot. The sun was piercing through some overhead tree branches, though it was still low in the sky, indicating that it had just risen.

Stanley's clothes were nowhere to be seen. He did have an abundance of junk around him, as though he'd tried to make a nest for himself. A dinosaur skull was the most notable find, resting at his feet. There was an empty gin bottle, a shovel, some chains and a folded up lawn chair. It looked as though he may have raided someone's garage or tool shed.

His tongue felt sticky, and his saliva was syrupy and metallic. It tasted like old blood. He spit onto the pavement and wiped his mouth on the back of his hand. The fear of what he may have done in the night was all-consuming.

He looked at his spit-smeared hand. It was not the hand of Nic Cage. His body was his own again as well. Cage had vanished. He was Stanley again. He was naked Stanley outdoors.

The lot he was in was full of new cars. He kept low to the ground, crouching as he scuttled to the back of the Mustangs along a fence line and peered out. A handful of cars drove past. There was a pizza place across the street that was still closed, which he recognized. He was easily a half hour walk from home.

Stanley found a discarded plastic bag under a bush along the fence line. It wasn't good for much and it wasn't going to stop people from staring if they saw him, but it was better than nothing. He tore two holes in it and pulled it on like a pair of underwear, then squatted in place for another moment, letting the humiliation simmer to a tolerable level.

"You can do this," he told himself, not believing it for a moment. And then he ran.

The sun had just barely risen, so he'd have no better time to get a move on. Most businesses were still closed and there were few people on the streets. He ran when the coast was clear, ducking behind parked cars and into alleyways and doorways as he picked his moments carefully. The plastic bag crinkled and crunched as he ran, the sound as loud as a marching band in his own mind. Despite his best efforts to remain unseen, he endured several yells and catcalls from drivers and a few pedestrians who caught sight of him.

When he reached home, the door was locked. More cars filled the streets, as did people out walking to work or school. He climbed atop the dumpster at the side of the building and scuttled up to the fire escape, jumping to reach the ladder and tearing a gash in his plastic bag underpants in the process. His humiliation was complete.

Refusing to look out at the street and those to whom he'd exposed himself, he returned to his own window and ducked into the safety of his apartment. He never wanted to go outside again. He would just chain himself to his own bed and live there forever, he decided. He could become an online gambler and Cameron could do all the shopping for him. It would work out fine.

He sat, naked and partially ensconced in a dirty trash bag, breathing heavily below his own window. His venture into the night had only made things worse. Dead police officers and a Dog Cage were not the things he had hoped to find at all. He was no closer to figuring out how to undo what had been done. If anything, he was now in a worse place. There were multiple Nic Cages. He had no idea which one had bitten him. There could have been dozens, maybe hundreds. And it was spreading. The man walking his dog had become Cage. Would the police who were attacked be next? Was anyone safe?

The idea that Nic Cage was spreading like a virus should have been the greatest absurdity in the world. And yet Stanley was faced with that fact. How long would it take? If one Nic Cage made two new Nic Cages in a night, how many days until everyone in town was Nic Cage? Until everyone in America was Nic Cage?

Stanley went to his computer and headed to Netflix, looking for the movie *The Thing*. It was the first movie he and Cameron had watched together as roommates. He skipped ahead to the scene where Wilford Brimley uses a terrible computer from the eighties to predict the end of the world. Three years. The Thing would take over the entire world in three years. Nic Cage had to be at least that fast. If Stanley couldn't figure out what happened and how to stop it, the world would end in three years.

He swore loudly, closing his computer.

"Hey, Stanley, you alright?" Cameron called from out in the apartment.

"I think the world is ending," he yelled back.

"Alright."

Cameron said nothing else, and Stanley scuttled to the bathroom. His body was covered in scratches, scrapes and mud. He looked like he'd spent the night wrestling shrubs in the nude. He couldn't keep living like that. Waking up in strange places every morning. Doing God knows what at night when his Cage instincts became too hard to resist.

He washed up quickly and got dressed, then returned to the computer. The lead story from the local news was about the park attack. Two officers were killed. Plus another person elsewhere in town who survived.

"The victim identified Hollywood actor Nicolas Cage as the assailant. Cage's spokespeople were unavailable for comment," Stanley read out loud. He touched the wound on his neck again, the edges crusty and still slightly warm to his fingers. Nic Cage turned him into a WereCage. And if not the real Cage, then someone down the line from the real one. Nic Cage must have bitten someone at some point when he was in town.

"Son of a bitch."

## Chapter Seven

Stanley tried everything he could think of on Google. He searched for "Nic Cage bites" and "Nic Cage bit me" and "Nic Cage werewolf." Nothing useful turned up that didn't relate to a Nic Cage movie. No one had ever called the police in real life to report being bitten by Nic Cage. There weren't even any conspiracy threads about it on Reddit or Twitter. Literally no one on the internet had been bitten by Nic Cage.

After an hour of desperate searching, Stanley even tried Bing and DuckDuckGo. It was not a Google conspiracy. Nic Cage just didn't bite people.

The only results anywhere were from that morning, in his town, in the article he'd just read. Aside from that, all Stanley could find were stories about Cage being vaguely weird in real life, which was one of the things Stanley liked about the man and none of which provided info he didn't already know.

It seemed obvious something had gone sideways in the world of Cage recently. Biting people wasn't his routine. And if they were attacking people with nightly regularity, then it was a phenomenon just a couple of days old. That was a clue, Stanley was sure.

Maybe Bitey Cage, the one that had bitten him in the park that night, was also Alpha Cage. Maybe that one was the first and Stanley was the second, barring, of course, the possibility that the real Nic Cage bit that first one at some point.

The idea that he was so unlucky as to be the first victim of anything, let alone Nic Cage lycanthropy, was not something Stanley had readily considered. Was it a good thing or a bad thing? Had to be good, he supposed. It meant the infection was still relatively contained and small.

There were too many things he didn't understand. Why were the other Cages so violent? He was mostly himself in Cage form. He didn't want to eat people. And though he had the urge to spout Cage quotes, he could resist and use his own words. What was the difference?

No one was going to answer his questions. Even Google, the smartest thing on the internet, couldn't answer his questions. That meant it was all on him. Stanley had to be smarter than the internet. There was no way. He opened a new window.

He Googled "lycanthropy but not werewolves." If not Nic Cage, surely somewhere had encountered a were-something before. Like a rabbit or a stevedore or something.

"Therianthropy," Stanley muttered, scrolling through the results. The ability to metamorphose into other animals, the most famous example of which was werewolves. So it was a thing. As much of a thing as werewolves were, anyway. The problem with that being they were generally considered fictional and still somehow sounded less crazy than a WereCage.

The link after therianthropy caught his attention. It was a page about clinical lycanthropy, a psychiatric condition in which a person thinks they're a werewolf. The first page was too in-depth, so he looked it up on Wikipedia instead. It was a rare disorder, and the afflicted suffered from delusions of lycanthropy.

Stanley looked at his own reflection in the laptop screen. He could be delusional. It almost made sense. Dead end job, no friends, childhood trauma, maybe an overabundance of fandom for Nic Cage. What if he was just insane?

He wasn't sure if mental illness was prevalent in his family, but maybe it didn't matter. He did live a weird life. Where was he going? He was an adult stock boy. Sometimes customers called him "boy" to his face. And he did have a rich and vivid imagination.

Stanley left the room, finding Cameron on the living room couch with his own laptop.

"Would you tell me if I was crazy?" he asked. Cameron glanced up at him.

"Your face is scratched to shit," he said.
"Would you?"
"Crazy how?" his roommate replied. Stanley raised an eyebrow.
"What does that mean?"
"Clinically, mental illness can take on any number of forms. Depression is a mental illness. I'm depressed, for God's sake. It's something you can deal with. But when you use a word like 'crazy,' which you shouldn't by the way, I feel like you mean full looney tunes. Like maybe psychotic or something. Is that what you mean?"
"I mean delusional," Stanley answered.
"Is this about Nic Cage?"
"Obviously."
"Hmm. Okay. In my opinion, that bite is not a delusion. But do I think Nic Cage bit you? I think -"
"I turned into Nic Cage," Stanley blurted out, surprising himself. The two roommates stared at each other for a moment in silence. Stanley suspected he may have looked even more surprised to have said it than Cameron was to hear it.
"Again?" Cameron said.
"After. At night. I turned into Nic Cage. I'm a werewolf. But not a wolf. Nic Cage. I'm WereCage."
Cameron very slowly closed his laptop and set it aside.
"Sit with me, Stanley," he said. Stanley tentatively sat on the sofa, on the far end, leaving an empty cushion between the two of them. "Tell me your story."
"I got bit by Nic Cage. Then at night I turned into Nic Cage. And I went to find the Nic Cage that bit me in the park, and there was a man and a dog and they were Nic Cage and they killed two police officers that took a selfie with me and I woke up in a used car lot."
"Stan, there's a whole lot in that run on sentence."
"Yeah," he agreed.
"Should I get us some wine?"
"It's not even nine in the morning," Stanley pointed out. Cameron got up and walked to the kitchen, taking a half bottle of Shiraz out of the fridge and two wine glasses from the cupboard. He poured them each a glass and then sat with his leg crossed and arm draped over the edge of the sofa arm, watching his roommate.
"Two police officers are dead?" he asked before taking a sip. Stanley nodded.
"And Nic Cage is a dog?"
"Dog Cage, I called him. And the other one was Raging Cage. Real angry guy. He killed the cops."
"Cute," Cameron said. "Names are fun."
"I'm not joking, Cam," Stanley said with all the seriousness he could muster.
Cameron took a long drink of his wine and set the empty glass on the coffee table.
"Tell me about becoming Nic Cage."
"I dunno what to say. It was at night. Full moon and all that, you know? I just turned into him and ran out the fire escape. I could hear his movie quotes in my head. And I wanted to break into the museum and stuff."
"You turned physically into him?"
"Fully."
"And there was a dog that was also Nic Cage?"
"He was just a tiny Nic Cage. He had a collar on."
"And a third guy who killed two cops?"
"It's on the news," Stanley said, gesturing to the computer.

"Is it, though?"

"The dead cops are," Stanley clarified.

Cameron leaned forward and put his hands on top of Stanley's.

"Stanley, I love you like a brother. Like a weird, introverted, lonely brother. I don't think you're crazy. But I do believe there is a greater than average chance you're suffering some kind of delusions and may need to seek the aid of a mental health professional."

"It's called clinical lycanthropy," Stanley told him. His roommate leaned back and took Stanley's glass of wine.

"What is?"

"The delusion where you think you're a werewolf. I thought maybe I had that, right? But you can see my bite, right? And the cops are really on the news. That really happened."

Cameron shrugged as he drank, offering Stanley a nod.

"Alright, well, the bite is real but it may be a stretch, as far as my understanding of biology goes, to proclaim that bite turned you into Nic Cage. In a real, literal sense. And the police thing may have just been, I don't know, drug mules. Maybe the bite triggered a delusion. What about that?"

"Yeah," Stanley said, touching his shoulder. "I could see that. Like maybe it was a hobo and his hobo mouth gave me brain parasites?"

"Okay," Cameron agreed. "Let's go with that for now."

Stanley took a deep breath. He felt stupid because he sounded stupid. But he sounded stupid because this was real to him. Even if Cameron was having some fun at his expense, it was good to say it out loud and try to wrap his head around it.

One of two things had to be true. Either he was suffering some kind of mental breakdown that had convinced him he turned into Nic Cage after being bitten by his favorite actor, or he was not suffering a mental breakdown and all of that was real. Neither of those choices made him feel good.

"You have to go talk to someone, I think," Cameron suggested.

"Goddamn it," he replied. The only thing worse than being a lycanthropic Nic Cage was the possibility he wasn't. Now he didn't even know for sure what his problem was. This was a huge step backwards.

"I could call someone?" Cameron offered. Stanley shook his head.

"No. I know someone. It's kind of weird, isn't it?"

"Oh, it's more than kind of weird," his roommate agreed. Stanley shook his head.

"No, I mean, I was almost hoping it was real for a second. Maybe I still am. Being a WereCage would be less awful than just thinking you were one, wouldn't it?"

Cameron finished the second glass of wine, studying Stanley's face carefully.

"That may be one of the most profoundly unanswerable questions I have ever heard."

"Yeah. Okay, I'm going to go. Thanks for not making fun of me too much."

Cameron smiled and patted his knee.

"That's what I'm here for," he told him.

Stanley headed back to his room and got his keys and phone, then did his best to make himself look presentable despite his scratched up face. He headed out and returned to the medical clinic on Belmont street.

Nurse Sara was working at the desk when he came in, and despite his situation, Stanley smiled. He got that sense of lightness in his chest when he saw her that made him think he was going to say something completely stupid and ruin his chances of impressing her forever. He'd only met one other girl before who gave him that feeling. Her name was Tina, and she was in his tenth grade French class. He'd said something completely stupid and ruined his chances of ever impressing her.

"Hey, look who's back. How's that shoulder?" she asked him as he approached the desk.

"It's good. It's better. It's bad," he answered.

"Interesting," she said, typing something on her computer. Then, leaning in and looking around the room at the other waiting patients, she lowered her voice in a conspiratorial fashion.

"I just saw on the news this morning someone else who said they were attacked by Nic Cage."

"Right?" he said too loudly, then winced and lowered his voice as well. "That's why I came in today!"

"Oh my God, did Nic Cage bite you again?" she asked. He shook his head.

"No, that wasn't me. But the whole Nic Cage thing. I need to talk to the doctor about that."

"Well, okay. I don't know that I can just write 'Nic Cage' in the note on your file, though. Is there a specific concern you have?"

"Clinical lycanthropy," he answered. She paused in her typing and narrowed her eyes.

"Is that a real thing or...?"

"You've never heard of it?" he asked.

"Can't say that I have. But you have."

"I Googled it," he replied. She smiled and continued typing.

"Doctor loves it when people Google stuff, he'll be excited by this one."

"Was that sarcastic?" he asked her. She nodded enthusiastically.

"Very much so. They hate when patients Google their symptoms. Had a lady in here last month who thought she had ebola after a nosebleed. It's wild stuff, let me assure you."

"I'm sorry, I don't want to be a... whatever you call that. A Googler."

Sara smiled at him.

"No. I'm sorry if I made you feel weird. It never hurts to be educated. But it's good you came in for a second opinion. I'm a Googler too. I support Googling."

Stanley laughed at that and then felt a rush of undeserved confidence roll over him. He was potentially on the brink of discovering that he was either a WereCage or suffering a debilitating mental illness. His life was in a state of flux like never before. He needed to seize the day.

"Maybe we can Google together sometime," he said. The words fell out of his mouth like a terrible, dark curse. He realized as he spoke them that he would have been better served just yelling gibberish like some kind of agitated gibbon. What man said such a thing to a woman? It was the exact opposite of smooth. It was rough. It was the roughest, worst pick up line anyone had ever uttered.

"Oh wow," she replied. He grimaced as another patient got into line behind him. Sara's expression could have been amused or baffled. He couldn't tell. Clearly, he was no longer able to trust his sense, anyway.

"Gonna sit," he said, heading to the chairs. He sat on the far side of the room and waited patiently in silence, watching a morning talk show on the muted TV. Sara glanced at him more than once and he averted his eyes each and every time, pretending to focus on his phone. He felt like he was being weak and stupid and childish, but mentally he wasn't sure he was in a good place. A bad pickup line was the last thing he needed to deal with on top of everything else.

Minutes passed with agonizing slowness. People were called in to see the doctor. New people showed up. Sara kept glancing at Stanley, and Stanley kept pretending he hadn't been looking at her. It was like a dance.

Finally, his time came. Sara called his name and stood at the entrance to the hallway, waiting for him. He approached with as much false confidence as he could muster.

"Saw you on your phone over there," she said to him quietly. "Looked like some intense Googling."

He sighed loudly, and she grinned, leading him down the hall to the exam room.

"In here. The doctor will be in shortly."

"Thank you," he said.

She left without another word. Stanley sat on the paper sheet-covered table again. Several minutes passed and then the doctor entered.

"Mr. Miller, hello," he said without looking up from a chart. "I just saw you about a bite, didn't I?"

"Yeah," Stanley agreed. The doctor looked at him finally and nodded.

"Right. Human bite. Is it alright?"

"Yeah. no. But yeah. I'm here about something else," he replied. The doctor nodded his head, giving the chart a slight shake.

"Nurse Wayland's note here says 'lycanthropy.' Please tell me that's incorrect."

"It is!" Stanley stated. "It's clinical lycanthropy, actually."

"Clinical lycanthropy. You have me at a loss, Mr. Miller."

"I Googled it -" he began, and though the doctor didn't say anything, his eyes definitely tightened at the corners when the word "Google" escaped Stanley's lips. "It's a psychiatric disorder. Where, you know, someone thinks they're a werewolf."

The doctor set the chart down on his desk and took a seat in the swivel chair.

"Okay, that's something I have never encountered. And you think you suffer from this?"

"Not exactly," Stanley stated. The doctor smiled unsurely.

"I'm a little confused then."

"You and me both," he replied. "I don't think I'm a werewolf exactly. I think I was bit by Nic Cage and then I turned into Nic Cage."

To his credit, the doctor held his neutral expression remarkably well. Just another quick tightening at the corner of the eyes. If not for the noticeably long, silent pause, it seemed like nothing unusual had transpired at all.

"Is there a reason for that?"

"The bite you treated, it was from Nic Cage," Stanley explained. "Like, I don't think it was really Nic Cage, I think it was another WereCage."

"WereCage is the word we're using?"

"I am, yeah," Stanley agreed.

"And so that person was bitten by Nic Cage, the actor?"

"Maybe. Okay, but I think it's more likely that didn't happen and that I'm imagining it. That makes more sense, right? Because I can't really be turning into Nic Cage at night, can I? Like, medically?"

"Medically? No, I don't think so," the doctor agreed.

"So am I crazy then?"

"Well, we don't use that label, but you may benefit from speaking to someone with a little more expertise in this area than me. I'm going to refer you to a psychiatrist, okay? But if you feel like this... issue is too much to handle, then you can go to the hospital and check yourself in for a seventy-two hour psychiatric observation, okay? Strictly voluntary, but they will keep an eye on you and you'll be able to talk to a psychiatrist on staff and maybe get some more intensive help. Sound good?"

"No? But I guess I need it. I think."

"Well, it never hurts to talk about things with people," the doctor stated. He was right, of course, but Stanley couldn't help but think he was being a little more condescending than he had been. It was bordering on that patronizing way people talk to someone when they think they're crazy. He asked for it, though. Literally, even.

The doctor filled out some paperwork on his computer while Stanley sat awkwardly in silence on his crinkly paper seat. When the doctor was done, he stood and opened the door.

"I've put in the referral, so you should get a call in a few days to confirm an appointment. In the meantime, try to just take it easy. Go for a walk in the park -"

"I got bit in the park," Stanley interrupted. The doctor frowned.

"Okay, don't go for a walk in the park. Take a bath. Read a book. Try to take care of yourself, avoid anything that stresses you out, and make sure you take that call for the referral when it comes in."

Stanley agreed to do those things and thanked the doctor. As he left the clinic, Sara caught him at the door, walking outside with him.

"Can you just... leave?" he said, pointing at the clinic. She had a jacket on over her scrubs and nodded her head.

"It's my break, don't worry," she said. "Where you headed?"

"Home," he answered, nodding down the street in a vague acknowledgement of where his building was.

"Cool. Walk with me," she said, heading out. He walked alongside her, unsure of what was happening, when she glanced at him, a serious look on her face.

"I believe you," she said.

"Huh?"

"I don't think you have a psychiatric condition," she clarified. "I believe you."

"Oh."

They walked past an antique store and Stanley looked at an old birdcage in the window, distracting himself for a moment.

"Why?" he said finally.

"Timeline doesn't make sense, I think," she explained. "You came in and said Nic Cage bit you. Then a day later, a complete stranger on the news has the same story. This isn't in your head."

"Medically?" Stanley asked. She made a face.

"What?"

"Is that your medical opinion?" he asked her. She laughed and shrugged her shoulders.

"Well, I'm not signing any official documents. This is just my opinion."

"So you think I'm a WereCage?" he asked her, keeping his eyes ahead instead of looking at her. In his peripheral vision, he could see her looking at him, though.

"Okay, I didn't say that. But you got bit by someone. So did someone else. You both think it was Nic Cage. So what if someone who looks like Nic Cage is literally out in the park at night attacking people? That, to me, is more plausible than you suffering some kind of lycanthropy."

"But I think I turned into a WereCage."

"You have to stop using that word," she told him. "But also, yeah, you got bit by a guy and then so did someone else. What does that tell you?"

Now he looked at her, having no idea where she was going.

"Both of you were bitten in the park on different nights. So this isn't a crazy person. Why not during the day? Why not dozens of people? This is a planned attack. Maybe they stuck you with something like LSD or mescaline or something."

"Mescaline?" he asked.

"Comes from cactus. Makes you feel all dreamy and sort of alters your perception."

"Huh," Stanley said. That was not what he felt like. He felt like Nic Cage. Because he was Nic Cage.

"That's about the best reply I could hope for," she told him, stopping at a corner in front of a Subway.

"I'm gonna go in here and get a sandwich, then I have to get back to work. Do you want to grab a coffee or something later today after I'm done?"

He was surprised by the question and paused for too long before answering. She frowned at him.

"Or not," she said. He shook his head.

"No. Yes. No! I'd love to," he stated.

"Give me your phone," she told him. He unlocked it and handed it over, and she put her number in his contacts.

"Now if you don't call, I'll know you're crazy," she said, handing the phone back.

"I didn't think we used that word."

"Oh, we'll use that word and more if you don't call me. I'm off at six, so do you want to meet up around seven?"

"Yes, I do," he agreed. She laughed at him and made her way into the Subway. Stanley took a right at the corner and headed downtown.

## Chapter Eight

Stanley had planned to head home after the clinic, but he felt like he needed to be elsewhere. He needed to be out in the world when he was still normal and mostly sane. In the light of day, he was still Stanley Miller. He didn't feel like he was lost in himself. He was solid and reliable, just like every day. He was him, and so he needed to take advantage of that.

Walking down the street and passing other people, watching cars stop and go, was something he'd always taken for granted. Just being a person in a crowd that no one paid attention to. But that morning it felt like he'd lost that normalness. He was naked and wounded and Nic Cage. It was weird and uncomfortable. So to be able to regain that feeling of being no one special was something he was actually enjoying.

He walked for blocks, wandering the heart of the city. The lunch rush was just beginning and the restaurants in the core were bustling. High school students, office workers and everyone else who could get away were darting in and out of burger joints, coffee shops and pizza places.

Stanley took a turn down an alley that had a ramen shop and a deli near the mouth and followed a trail of unusual smells and lights to the front of a store that was lit up with tiny lanterns. A buzzing neon sign in the window advertised tarot readings and psychic predictions.

There was no actual name on the business, and it was in a squat little yellow brick location with a bright red door at the end of the alley. It was ticking all the cliche boxes Stanley felt a psychic needed.

"What the hell?" he said out loud. He pushed on the red door, causing a bell to jangle, and stepped inside.

The interior of the shop was very small but open and dimly lit. There was a round table in the center of the room draped with a long white tablecloth. A deck of cards sat in the center.

Two of the walls were adorned with shelves full of herbs and books and crystals and more mystical items that Stanley couldn't identify. The room smelled vaguely of spices, maybe some kind of incense. He couldn't place the odor, but it reminded him of cookies.

There was a beaded curtain at the back wall that parted a moment after Stanley entered, revealing a middle-aged woman with hair as red as copper and green eyes that had to be faked with contact lenses.

"Have you come for a reading?" she asked, inviting Stanley to sit. The chair was rickety and lightweight and reminded him of school chairs for children. He sat precariously.

"Maybe?" he answered. She sat across from him in a chair designed for adults, giving him a thoughtful look as she eyed him up and down.

"I am Madame Maleva. You are?"

"Stanley Miller," he said, extending his hand. "I've had a weird couple of days."

"The days grow weirder for many," she agreed, shaking his hand very delicately. "Let's see what the cards say, yes?"

"Yeah, sure. Do I need to do anything?"

"The cards can give you answers, but that means you need to ask a question. What do you wish to know today, Stanley Miller?"

"What's happening to me?" he said without hesitation. It was a vague question, but it cut to the heart of the matter. Madame Maleva smiled at him and nodded her head. She picked the deck of cards off of the table and began to shuffle.

"Tell me about what brings you here," she said, shuffling the deck and watching him carefully.

"Like, exactly what brought me here?" he asked. She gave a half-hearted shrug.

"The cards will offer more answers if they understand what you need. You want to know what's happening to you? Tell me about it, why it concerns you, what you hope to learn about this period in your life."

"You're going to think I'm crazy," he told her. She laughed lightly.

"People think I am crazy all the time," she countered.

"It's just... something happened to me recently. And now I don't know if I can even trust myself anymore. For more than one reason. Maybe a thing happened and now nothing makes sense. Or maybe it didn't happen and I'm just confused."

Madame Maleva didn't slow her shuffling at all and her expression didn't waver in the slightest. Instead, she continued the shuffle a moment longer and set the deck before him.

"Take the cards, but do not look at them," she instructed. Stanley did as he was told, holding the overly large cards in both hands.

"Shuffle them," she instructed. He did so, sliding the cards into one another but keeping his eyes off of them. After a brief moment, she reached for them.

"That will do. Please," she said. He handed them back, and she held them for a moment, closing her eyes in silence. She placed the deck before him again.

"Clear your mind and split the deck into three piles, then put them back together," she instructed. He did as he was told and then she reached for the deck, drawing it back in front of her.

"Let us see what the cards have to say about your unique condition."

"That's one word for it," Stanley said. She laughed and drew a card, placing it face up on the table. The image depicted was a skeletal man enshrouded in darkness. The text on the bottom read "Death."

"Seriously?" he muttered. Madame Maleva's smile was coy.

"The Death card is very misunderstood. Death is rarely literal in this sense, but transitory. A change, moving from one life to another."

She flipped over the next card and the image was a clear, bright yellow moon.

"The moon signifies illusion. Perhaps deception. It can indicate a lie even from yourself, or confusion that has led you astray."

"I'll buy that," Stanley stated. Madame Maleva flipped another card over. The final card depicted a man who looked as though he were about to walk off a cliff. A dog barked at his heels and he carried a bindle staff, although this card was upside down compared to the others.

"The Fool," Madame Maleva said. Stanley frowned, feeling that was a bit too on the money for him.

"The reverse Fool," she clarified. "This signifies a risk, a reckless one at that. It could indicate a kind of gullibility. Perhaps you are walking into something dangerous with blinders on."

"This doesn't sound promising," he told her. She gave another half shrug at that.

"You are at a crossroads in your life and the path forward is not clear. You face a transition, a time of change, and you stand at the precipice of proceeding down a dangerous path. Or a fruitful one. Danger is not guaranteed. You may find that great risk brings great reward if you are both brave and smart about how to proceed."

"So what can I do?" he asked. She looked at the cards again, then back at him.

"The cards offer answers, but not solutions. What you do is up to you. But know that your fate is not sealed. Your path need not be one you fear."

Stanley stared at the three cards again. Death, the Moon and the Fool. He was almost surprised Death didn't have Nic Cage's face. He looked up and Maleva was staring deeply into his eyes. It made him feel uncomfortable, but he held her gaze until she began to speak.

"Why are you here, Stanley Miller?" she asked. He took a deep breath and tried to consider the best way to explain himself.

"What do you know about lycanthropy?" he said.

"Whoever is bitten by a werewolf and lives becomes a werewolf themselves," she stated plainly. "Victims of the wolf will be freed from its curse when the source of the curse is killed." Then she narrowed her eyes. "But you were not bitten by a wolf."

"How do you know that?" he asked.

"I'm psychic," she said. There was a silence between them after that, and Stanley couldn't tell if she was joking or not.

"Draw a card from the top of the deck and place it before you," she told him. "You will draw two cards and they will help you determine how to proceed."

He reached for the deck and slid the top card off, then flipped it over onto the table. The image was of a man and a woman embracing, their eyes cast up to the heavens. The text on the bottom read "The Lovers."

"One more," Madame Maleva said. He did as he was told, placing a card depicting a bearded man on a throne. The name was "The Emperor."

"Your path is not clear," she said, looking at the cards. "A powerful figure stands in your way. To overcome their influence, you cannot go alone. Harmony and stability will come with the guiding influence of another. Together, you will achieve your desired goal. But if you go alone, it may not."

"What do I need to do?" he asked.

"You need to act. Your life is mired in inaction. Self-doubt. Fear and trepidation. You have simmered for too long, never wanting to take the next step. It is time to do so."

"I have no idea what that means," he told her. She smiled, and it was warm if somewhat disbelieving.

"You absolutely know what it means."

Stanley tried mulling that over for a moment and was tempted to point out, again, he didn't know what that meant, either. He chose to keep that to himself instead.

"Do you want to know what really happened to me?" he asked, not meeting her eyes this time. Someone who was psychic, or at least claimed to be psychic, seemed like they'd be at least open to the idea of Nic Cage lycanthropy.

Maleva leaned forward, placing a hand over his own on the table. He lifted his gaze and met her eyes once more. The spice smell in the room had all but faded away.

"No," she said to him. "I don't need to know."

Stanley looked at the moon card, and the Fool. Was he the fooled? Or was he acting foolish? Or was everything some kind of cosmic joke?

"Is any of this for real?" he asked her. She drew her hand back, still smiling that faint, mysterious smile.

"What do you consider real?" she asked him in return.

"Stuff I can see and feel and so can other people. Stuff that happens whether I'm here or not."

"Are dreams not real, then? Your hopes and desires? No one else sees or feels those."

"I'm way beyond hopes and dreams here. Nightmares, maybe."

"Just as real," she told him.

Stanley took a deep breath. He was as afraid of being crazy as he was of being sane. He was afraid he was going to die.

"I just want everything back the way it was," he said then. She shook her head, collecting the cards from the table.

"No one gets to have things the way they were and do you know why?" she said. He did not and offered a slight shake of his head by way of an answer.

"Because things are the way they are. Tomorrow is what they will be. But what they were was yesterday, and you can never go back. No one can."

"That's some real fortune cookie stuff," he told her. She smiled at that, a bright and genuine smile.

"Fortune cookies aren't real, though."

Stanley got to his feet. He paid her twenty-five dollars for her time before heading back out into the alley once more. He felt armed with even less understanding than he had before he came in, but also a tentative sense of calm. He couldn't go back. Whatever happened, he had to move into it, not away from it. Because there was no away. There never would be.

Outside, the day was growing warmer. He called in to work and told them he'd been up all night vomiting and wouldn't be able to come in. Whether Madame Maleva knew anything or was just blowing smoke up his ass didn't really matter. He was in the same boat either way. He couldn't keep doing things the same way, not if he wanted to figure out what had happened and what he could do about it.

There was only one place he could think to go. He had to return to the park. In the light of day, he could be himself and stay himself. He could see if anything was unusual, maybe find some kind of clue or evidence that could explain what was happening.

If all the attacks were happening in the park, he thought there was a good chance that the other Cages might go there, too. They'd be their real selves, their non-Cage selves, but surely they were all looking for answers as well. Maybe he and the others could meet up and pool their resources to figure out what was going on. There was no way the rest of them wanted to be afflicted any more than he did. Or at least he hoped that was the case.

He tried to keep focused on the immediacy of what he was doing as he returned to the park. Walking down the street, waiting at stoplights, watching cars go by. No need to think about little Nic Cage dogs or the possibility of living his life as a monster.

*Was that even the right word? Monster?* He wasn't sure. Nic Cage wasn't necessarily a monster. But what was happening to him had no real explanation that wasn't going to be at least a little monstrous.

The park looked like a totally different place in the light of day, all green and vibrant and normal. There were people walking dogs, none of which looked like Nic Cage, and the sights and sounds of everyday life were all around.

The park was located dead center in the middle of the city and took up what would have been the equivalent of at least fifteen blocks. Maybe more, Stanley's sense of spatial understanding was limited at best. He had a concept of what an acre was, but he had no way to guess in practical terms how large it might have been. It didn't matter, though. The park was big. That was what mattered.

From picnic areas to the pond to a splash pad and a small forest, it had a lot of serene, outdoorsy type stuff that was good for making you feel like you weren't being choked to death by steel and concrete. Stanley didn't go there often enough to know his way around it very well.

He wandered through an entrance far from where he was attacked, close to a band shell that was used for outdoor concerts and summer festivals. Despite the early hour on a weekday, there were a good number of people in the park just walking and relaxing. It was as though no one had a job or the awareness that people had been killed there the night before.

If nothing else, the number of people casually wandering the park ensured he wouldn't look suspicious doing the same. He made his way towards where the police had stopped him, circumnavigating the pond and cutting through the trees down a bicycle path. He tried to look for signs of anything suspicious on his way, like footprints or maybe some kind of blood spatters, but he also realized how dumb that was. There were footprints everywhere and he couldn't imagine why blood spatters would be in the middle of nowhere.

The bike path led out to a crossroads and a main thoroughfare that connected with the path he'd walked the night before. After several minutes of walking, he could see that a large section of the park was cordoned off and police were protecting the area. Maybe they were looking for their own footprints and blood spatters. Maybe they'd already made plaster casts of Stanley's feet and had surly German shepherd dogs ready to track his scent and tear his lungs out.

He circled wide around where the police were, not wanting to draw attention to himself, and instead headed around to where he thought Dog Cage and Raging Cage had come from.

The police on the scene had a number of tiny things on the ground marked by small, white placards and were actively searching through weeds off the path. Stanley picked up a mushroom growing next to a tree without any idea if it was edible or poisonous. If anyone asked, he was an urban forager. It seemed like it was stupid enough to be believable.

He wandered off the path, clutching his mushroom and trying not to look at the police. He was far enough away that none of them were paying him much mind, not that they had any reason to suspect him of anything, anyway. They weren't looking for anyone who looked like him.

Beyond the path were more trees in a small cluster that ran close to the border of the entire park. It was a place where people sometimes sat to get away from the summer sun or to feed the squirrels.

There was a depression in amongst a group of maple trees that was wet and muddy. In the center there was a clear footprint from a man's shoe which, alone, meant nothing. But the very tiny human footprints next to it were what drew Stanley's attention. They had to be from Dog Cage.

Stanley took out his phone and snapped a quick picture of the footprints. He stood over them for a long moment, excited to have found some evidence of what had happened until it occurred to him it proved nothing. So Dog Cage had feet. That was hardly a revelation.

It wasn't as though he could go tell the police what he'd found. Little footprints in the mud. So what? That and his mushroom would make him look like an idiot. But he could tell Cameron about it. And maybe Sara. Someone had to believe him. And maybe they could help him think of what to do next. Otherwise, he'd end up coming back to the park every day and accomplishing nothing.

Madame Maleva told him he couldn't go back. And there he was, back in the park. Of course he wasn't going to find anything there. He needed to move forward. Not just with Cage, but with everything. He needed to go. Home to Cameron. Then dinner with Sara. And then figure this Cage thing out and get his life back on track.

Those little footprints were like an accusing finger, pointing the way to his own failure to figure anything out. Not just now, but for years. Since his family fell apart. Since he went off to college. Since he started drifting at a snail's pace towards nothing.

Stanley threw his mushroom on the ground. He didn't need to fake being a forager. He'd been faking everything in his life. He was a full grown man stocking shelves in a grocery store because it was so easy he could do it with his brain off. He was a man with no ambition. And now he was standing at the precipice of losing everything before he had anything.

If he was losing himself, if he was at risk of dying or killing others or being Patient Zero from some kind of Nic Cage pandemic, what did he have to show for himself? He wasn't even a man losing the things he loved. He had never even gained anything.

Stanley had no idea if that was better or worse than losing a life that actually had meaning. Was a guy with a career and a love life and some sense of happiness worth more than he was? Or was the fact that Stanley still had the potential to get all that even more valuable? He was at the beginning of the trip, not in the middle. Or he would be, if he didn't get gnawed on by a late night Nic Cage monster like his neck was a half price chicken wing at Stuckey's Bar and Tavern.

"Goddamn it," he muttered to himself. If he died now, or became Nic Cage permanently, or the whole world ended, it wouldn't even matter. He'd done literally nothing of merit with his life at all. He couldn't let himself go out like that.

## Chapter Nine

Cameron was making grilled cheese when Stanley returned home. The apartment had that tasty fried smell that didn't really smell like any food at all, so much as a frying pan that had something cooking in it, but it still made his mouth water.

"Did you get fired for telling people you were Nic Cage?" Cameron asked before he'd closed the door.

"What?" Stanley asked. Cameron was at the stove, flipping the sandwich over in the pan before taking a drink of what looked to be a margarita.

"Didn't your shift start like twenty minutes ago?"

"I called in sick," he explained.

"Are you sick? Did the doctor tell you that you have a brain parasite?"

"He referred me to a psychiatrist," Stanley answered. "But Sara believed me."

"Sara?" Cameron asked.

"The nurse at the clinic. We have a date later."

"Your life has been picking up a head of steam these last twenty-four hours. Why does the nurse believe your story?"

He flipped the grilled cheese over again and took a sip of his drink.

"Timing," Stanley answered. "She saw the story on the news about the other attack. It can't be in my head if it happened to someone else."

"Huh," Cameron said, taking the sandwich out of the pan. "But if you were really, you know, unwell, couldn't all of this be in your head?"

He began slicing the sandwich and then added a squirt of ketchup to the middle of the plate between the halves. Stanley frowned, watching the red sauce erupt from the squeeze bottle with an overtly farty sound.

"What do you mean 'all this' could be in my head? Like this conversation even?"

Cameron grabbed his plate and drink and walked around the kitchen island towards the living room. Stanley followed him.

"Not that I'm suggesting I'm a delusion, but if you're delusional, you can't really pick and choose what parts of your life are real and which are in your head. You'd never know."

"So you're suggesting you could be a delusion," Stanley clarified. His roommate sat on the sofa and then picked up half of his sandwich, dipping a corner in the ketchup before taking a bite. He chewed and shook his head before answering.

"I don't think I'm a delusion. But if I was, I might say the same thing. I think this is Cartesian philosophy."

"I never took philosophy. What the hell does that mean?"

"Listen," Cameron began, pointing a ketchup corner at him. "It doesn't matter. You have a date, that's great. And she thinks you're Nic Cage."

"She doesn't think I'm Nic Cage."

"But she doesn't think you're delusional," Cameron said, though it wasn't a question. He took another bite and watched Stanley expectantly.

"She's open-minded."

"And cute?" Cameron asked. "I picture like a young Charlize Theron, with a little sass and good upper body strength."

"Why are you picturing that?" Stanley wanted to know. He'd said her name, and that she was a nurse. Cameron was sometimes too caught up in his own head.

"I have a rich inner life, Stan. And I like this Sara. She's a critical thinker. I looked up the story too, about the Nic Cage attack. It's not long on details, but look at this."

He took his phone off of the table next to his plate and swiped on something, then turned it around. The image was a selfie, saturated by the light of the flash against a darkened background. It was the red-headed police officer, Walsh, with his arm around Nicolas Cage. Or, rather, Stanley."

"Oh wow, they released that?" Stan asked. Cameron shook his head.

"Cop put it on his Insta last night. I saw it about an hour ago and for the last hour, I've been drinking homemade margaritas in anticipation of having several more before I saw you next," his roommate admitted. Stanley narrowed his eyes.

"Why?" he asked. Cameron turned the phone around.

"Because I need you to look at this photo and tell me that's not your shirt Nic Cage is wearing," he said, taking another sip of his drink. Stanley looked at the picture. That was his shirt, the now missing shirt he'd lost somewhere between that photo and waking up naked in the morning.

"Oh," Stanley said, not sure of what else to say. Cameron's face dropped along with his phone as he shook his head, gulping down a mouthful of vibrant, green margarita from the log-stemmed cup.

"Oh God, Stanley. I was really hoping maybe you were delusional. It'd be a fun quirk and you need one. You're very dull. But this? This is you, isn't it?" His voice was tinged with panic. Stanley nodded.

"Yeah," he admitted.

"Thinking you're Nic Cage is adorable. I could remind you to take your pills and drive you to your appointments sometimes. I could do that. But being Nic Cage? Stanley, you're Nicolas Goddamn Cage. I don't know what to do with that."

He finished the first half of his sandwich, chewing aggressively.

"I'm sorry?" Stanley replied.

"We're all sorry, Stanley. The whole town is sorry. Did you eat this poor police officer's face off? Oh God, *Face/Off*," Cameron uttered, taking another drink.

"That wasn't me! I told you, it was Raging Cage and Dog Cage."

"The little Nic Cage dog. Oh, Stanley, we need to do something. You need to do something. Who do we call about this?"

Cameron was not a man who dealt with stress well. Part of the reason they had made such good roommates was that neither one of them ever did anything exciting. Cameron's life was nearly completely virtual. He'd suffered a lot of anxiety in college and found that working online and keeping to himself was a good way to avoid the stress of life. He wasn't agoraphobic, exactly. He just didn't want to go anywhere or do anything if he didn't have to. Things that upset his routine upset him as well.

"I don't think there are people you can call about this," Stanley told him.

"Then it's up to us. Mostly you. You can't go around eating police officers, Stanley. It's bad karma. Even if they're bad cops."

"I didn't kill those guys," Stanley pointed out again. "I was just playing along with them. They thought I was Nic Cage and so we chatted. And then the others showed up and went crazy."

Cameron finished his drink, watching Stanley through narrow, suspicious eyes.

"Okay, so the man and his little dog are both homicidal Nicolas Cages?"

"Seems like," Stanley agreed.

"But you're not," his roommate stated. Not quite a question, but Stanley felt there was a hint of one in there.

"Of course not!"

Cameron held his chin in his hand and studied Stanley closely.

"But that's weird, isn't it? Why are they killers and you're not? Why are any of you killers? Nicolas Cage never murdered anyone, did he?"

"No, never," Stanley agreed. If Nic Cage had killed someone, surely it would have made the news.

"Well, why would someone turn into Nic Cage and then kill a cop? Or bite you, for that matter? There's more mystery here than it seems, Stan."

"I don't think any of this is supposed to make sense."

"Everything makes some kind of sense. Even if we can't figure it out. Tell me what happens when you turn into Nic Cage."

Cameron's panic had faded like fog in the sunlight. Stanley suspected it had something to do with the number of margaritas he had consumed, but it didn't matter. He was onto something. A werewolf attacking people made sense, or as much sense as a human turning into a wolfman could. Wolves were predators. A big, man-sized wolf would still be a predator. Nic Cage was an actor. He shouldn't be attacking people.

"It's painful," Stanley explained. "The change hurts. Feels like my bones all break and muscles get ripped up. But then when it's done, it was like... I couldn't stop thinking in quotes from his movies. And everything seemed too real."

"What does that mean?" Cameron wanted to know.

"Things smell sharper. Look brighter. I felt stronger. But it was a struggle to keep my own thoughts sometimes. It's like all this random Nic Cage trivia and stuff rolls through your head and you have to push it away to keep focused."

"Nic Cage or Nic Cage characters?" Cameron asked.

"Oh. Characters, I guess," Stanley said. He hadn't considered the difference before, but he did seem to want to quote movies. And the others were quoting movies as well.

"That could be something. Nic Cage plays weird dudes, Stanley. If you're possessed by all of his characters or something, then you've got a big ol' fruit cocktail of maniacs in your head, don't you?"

"He's usually the good guy," Stanley said weakly.

"I watched him have a chainsaw fight in a movie once," Cameron countered. That was true as well. "And he had a flaming skull in two separate films."

"One's a sequel. That doesn't count."

"My point stands. If this condition is more about the characters than the actor, then that's a tad unstable, don't you think?"

"Yes, I do think that, Cameron," Stanley agreed. There was a little more to it than that, which made him feel it was unstable, but that was an okay start.

"I think you should call the police," Cameron told him. The statement took Stanley by surprise. He didn't think Cameron was the kind of person to rely on police to fix a problem. Not like this, anyway. If he told the police he was the Nic Cage in the photo, they'd probably lock him up forever.

"How will that help?"

"I don't know. There have to be scientists and stuff. Doctors. People who specialize in Nic Cage. They could give you radiation therapy or something," Cameron suggested. Stanley did not think any of that was likely to exist at the police station. And even if they did send him to a hospital, they'd probably just experiment on him. That's what happened in movies and he had become a movie star. It almost made too much sense.

Stanley had no desire to be locked in a room while scientists probed his orifices every time a full moon arrived. His plan was to take control of his life, not lose control of it.

"This is serious, Stanley. People are dead. You can't just shrug it off. You need help," Cameron insisted.

"I know that," he agreed. "I just don't think the police are the right answer."

"And what if you end up killing someone?" he suggested. Stanley could see the fear in his eyes, thinly masked thanks to the amount he'd had to drink. It made him nervous. The last thing he needed was Cameron ratting him out to the cops, thinking he was saving him from himself.

"I'll call," Stanley lied.

"Will you?" his roommate asked. Stanley nodded his head.

"I will. I just want all of this to be over. But I'm not missing my date with Sara. I'll call them in a few days when I've had time to process everything."

"A few days?" Cameron said.

"It's fine. The full moon is over. We have a whole month. I'll get it worked out."

"A month?" Cameron asked dubiously. Stanley stood up, anxious to be done with the conversation. He was hoping for his roommate to be more helpful and level headed, but he was in Margaritaville and would be of no use for some time.

"Not a whole month, I swear. Thanks, Cam," she said, turning away and heading towards his room.

"Promise me you won't eat me, Stanley," he shouted after him.

"Promise," Stanley replied, closing his bedroom door behind him. That was one ally essentially down. The only person he had left to rely on to figure out how to fix whatever had happened to him was now Sara, and he barely knew her at all.

He spent the remainder of the afternoon in the darkness of his room. He watched YouTube videos and read old comic books and tried to do what he thought a normal guy might do on a day off.

His mind wandered to the night in the park when he'd first been attacked. Who had that Cage been? Just another hapless victim like himself? Some random park goer in the wrong place at the wrong time? Was he still stalking the park at night? Stanley wished he had more insight into what was going on.

Despite Cameron's inebriated panic, he did bring up a good point. Stanley himself had not been overcome with an urge to kill anyone, so why were Raging Cage and Dog Cage doing that? They could have just been naturally aggressive, but that seemed a little over the top. And Bitey Cage was the same. Three other Cages had attacked people. Stanley had attacked no one. Was there some meaning in that?

He wondered if it had something to do with the nature of the attack. He'd heard the man walking his dog was killed. Stanley hadn't been killed, though, just bitten. Maybe if the attack had been more aggressive, he would have become more aggressive himself.

It occurred to him then that the two police officers were likely going to return at some point as well. No one knew what happened to them except Stanley. The police would think they were truly dead, but if they were WereCages, then they'd be able to return, probably. It happened to the man and his dog. Or maybe not. Maybe they were too badly killed, like how you can shoot a vampire and it won't die but stake it in the heart and it will die. And since it was a month until the next full moon, they'd just rot away like any corpse.

Stanley sat up in his bed. What if they were zombie WereCages now? Undead actors feasting on flesh. That would be even worse.

He checked the time and realized it was just after six. He scrolled through his contacts and found Sara's number where she'd put it in earlier in the day. He pressed the little green icon on his phone and held it to his ear.

"Hello?" came Sara's voice after one ring. He smiled and felt more relaxed.

"Hey, Sara, it's Stanley."

"Who?" she asked. The smile slipped from his lips.

"Stanley. From earlier today?"

"Gonna need more than that," she told him.

"Oh. I got bit by Nic Cage."

"Not ringing a bell," she replied. He blinked, dumbfounded to silence, and Sara snorted a laugh through the phone.

"I'm messing with you, Stanley. You're very prompt. It's literally three minutes after six."

"Oh, sorry. I thought -"

"No, it's cool. No time to waste," she said. He smiled again, relieved he hadn't messed up anything.

"I was checking to see if you still wanted to get dinner tonight," he said.

"Yeah, for sure. Do you like Chinese?" she asked.

"Yeah, Chinese is good." He hadn't had Chinese food in at least five years, but he was not opposed to it.

"Do you know Golden Wok on Fifteenth Street?"

"I don't," he answered.

"Well, time to put those Googling skills to work. It's on Fifteenth Street. Easy to find. Do you want to meet there at seven?"

He looked at his watch. It was now four minutes after six.

"I can do that," he told her.

"I can do it as well. Look at us go," she said. He was stuck in silence again for a moment, unsure of how to respond, and she laughed once more.

"I gotta run, get changed into something that hasn't been around sick people all day. I'll see you in an hour," she said.

"Yeah, no, yeah. For sure. Looking forward to it. Sounds like good. Good stuff," he said. She laughed again, and the phone went dead. He kept it to his ear for a beat longer, then lowered it, smiling as he looked at her number on his phone display.

He went to his closet and rifled through his wardrobe, trying to decide on what looked both presentable, yet sexy. He never bought clothes with the intent of being sexy in his life, so literally nothing fit the bill. He dropped sexy as a criterion and focused on presentable. He just needed to look like he cared and wasn't weird, although that ship had probably long since sailed. Still, dinner had been her idea, so it wasn't as though he'd put his foot in his mouth just yet.

He selected a navy blue button down shirt with a charcoal gray stripe down the left side and a pair of dark-colored pants. He didn't know if they qualified as slacks or trousers. Maybe they were just pants. The urge to Google the difference rose up, and he pushed it aside. He would not Google pants types. It didn't matter. They were pants, and they looked normal.

"Do these pants look normal?" he asked, leaving his room. Cameron was still on the sofa, working away on his computer. He had refreshed his margarita at some point. Probably more than once.

His roommate lifted his head above his laptop screen and scanned Stanley from head to toe.

"You look like someone's dad who's chaperoning a trip to a roller rink."

"Is that bad?" Stanley asked.

"Is this for your date with the nurse?"

"Yeah. We're getting Chinese."

"Your idea or hers?"

"Hers," Stanley said. Cameron narrowed his eyes.

"It's acceptable. Did you call the police?"

"I will later," he reminded him. "I want to do this date first without worrying about a SWAT team assault."

"Understandable," Cameron said, his voice a little slurry. He had drunk enough to pass beyond his initial worry and now seemed very relaxed.

"Is it safe for you to work drunk?" Stanley asked. Cameron rolled his eyes.

"My whole industry is drunk. This is fine."

"Okay. Well, I'm going to head out now, so I'm not late."

"Good choice, Stan. You can't afford to be late. And you say this woman knows the Nic Cage story?"

"She does, yeah."

"Hold on to her like grim death, my friend. In the entire time I've known you, I have never seen you date. This is big."

"I dated in college," Stanley protested. Cameron was no longer looking at him.

"Of course you did. We all did things in college. Don't eat this girl's face off."

"That wasn't me," he reminded Cam.

"Don't be late."

Stanley grunted, making sure he had his wallet before heading out. He really had dated in college. Not a lot, but it happened. And nothing since, really. He had a girlfriend online for a while, but she ended up hooking up with her ex and getting married over a weekend without telling Stanley it happened until a month later.

The turmoil of meeting a girl who was both interesting and pretty on top of the Nic Cage issue was more than he was used to dealing with. But maybe that was a good thing. Madame Maleva said he needed some help in figuring out how to move forward. Maybe Sara was the key to figuring his problems out. She was the only person in his corner right now. That couldn't have been a coincidence.

"I don't know when I'll be back," he told Cameron. His roommate didn't bother to respond. He locked the door behind himself and headed out.

Halfway to the restaurant, he regretted the decision to walk. He was getting sweaty and feared that he'd be glistening and smelly when he showed up. It would have made a terrible impression. He took the button down shirt off and held it as he walked, trying to keep cool.

It was just over a half hour to reach the restaurant from his apartment. The sky was slashed with color from the setting sun and there was a slight breeze that was finally cutting through the heat he felt. Stanley had always been more of a "dinner at five" kind of guy, and eating after sunset always made him feel like he had somehow messed up his scheduling. He didn't understand how people in movies were always having dinner dates at eight or nine o'clock. What did people do between getting home from school or work and such late dinners? He had no idea.

The Golden Wok looked to be a very small restaurant set into a strip of many restaurants that stretched several blocks. The outside was all gold and red, and there was a large cat statue at the host stand inside the door that had a mocking smile on its face as its hand bobbed back and forth as if to say hello.

Stanley stood on the street and put his button down shirt back on, looking through the window. He didn't see Sara inside, but he was a few minutes early, which was just as well. He had time to go to the washroom and splash some water on his face, maybe even get a cold drink to help cool off a little.

The last vestiges of the sun's light were hidden beyond the buildings of the city and only faint traces of purple and dark blue filled the partially cloudy sky. Stanley looked at his own reflection in the pane of glass and froze, his hands stuck forcing a button through a buttonhole in his shirt front.

His hairline was off, further back than it should have been. He shook his head and winced as a painful cramp struck him deep in his guts. A loud moan escaped his lips and a couple walking further up the sidewalk glanced in his direction.

Gritting his teeth, he swore under his breath. The pain blossomed behind his eyes and he felt like his skull was being pushed open from the inside.

Stanley stumbled away from the restaurant, clutching his stomach as he tried to maintain his balance. Other pedestrians gave him a wide berth, with only a handful pausing to ask if he was okay. He tried to wave them away, assure them it was nothing, but he couldn't form words. He groaned and growled and finally barked, "Papa's got a brand new bag!"

His vision swam, and he felt sick to his stomach. He scrambled down the street, stumbling into walls and windows. A sour taste filled his mouth, and his eyes and nose watered profusely. He felt like he was dying.

A man in a leather jacket said something to him that he couldn't make out as his eyes drifted up. The sky was black now, the last light of day just a memory. The sun was gone and the waning moon was partially covered by clouds. It wasn't full any longer. It wasn't supposed to do this.

*This isn't how werewolves work*, he thought, collapsing in an alley between a vape shop and a variety store. But he wasn't a werewolf, was he?

Bone popped in his back, and he screamed, using his own fist to muffle it. His knees and elbows shifted, his skull buckled and then reshaped itself inside of his own flesh. It felt like rats were moving inside of his body. Seconds felt like agonizing hours until finally the pain began to subside and he felt a stillness settle over him. Nothing moved or snapped or quivered inside. He was finished. It was finished.

He opened his eyes and stared up at the faint slash of sky visible between the buildings on either side of him. He could smell cooking smells and garbage. His heart was thudding like a drum solo, and his mind raced just as fast. Quotes from Nic Cage movies jumbled with his own thoughts, and he fought to push them aside.

Stanley got to his feet, still feeling unsteady, and braced himself on the alley wall. He watched clouds pass over the moon and cursed out loud. It was going to keep happening. Whatever had happened, it was not governed by the moon like some kind of story. It happened with the setting of the sun. Or maybe it was just any moonlight. It didn't matter. It wasn't over.

Somewhere out in the night, over the din of cars and pedestrians and the crush of city sounds, a cry reached Stanley's ears. He recognized the voice just as he recognized the words.

"I could eat a peach for hooooooooooouuuuuuuuuuuurs!" Nic Cage yelled. A distant Cage. Stanley couldn't place where it had come from, and had no way of knowing which of the other Cages it might have been. But the cry pulled at him. He felt it like a physical force, like a longing deep in his gut. It flipped his insides as though he were on a rollercoaster and he stood at the mouth of the alley.

"I just stole fifty cars in one night," he yelled back as loudly as he could. People on the street turned to see the source of the proclamation, but he turned away quickly, covering his own mouth as he ducked to the shadows of the alley again. He couldn't let anyone see him. Couldn't let them know Nic Cage was out and about once more.

His clothes no longer fit correctly and the urge to do preposterous and spontaneous things was creeping into the corners of his mind already. He needed to get back home. He wanted to wait for Sara, to show her for a fact that he was the thing he told her he was. But at the same time, he didn't want anyone to see, least of all her. The other Cages had hurt people, and he was feeling the loss of control more powerfully than before now. He feared what he might do if he was with her. Feared he might not be able to hold on to himself and end up hurting her as a result. He couldn't let that happen. He needed to get somewhere secure. Back in his room, locked up and away from anyone.

Stanley began reciting the order of the cans on the shelf at work. Green beans, sweet peas, peas and carrots, niblet corn, creamed corn, canned potatoes. On and on and on, repeating them when he got to the end. He'd stock the shelves a thousand times. He could navigate the store blindfolded if he had to. He tried to keep his mind on it, to ignore the urges to recite lines or find a dinosaur skull that tickled at his thoughts. He was Stanley Miller. He would always be Stanley Miller.

He ran down the alley, heading to Fourteenth Street, muttering under his breath the whole way.

"Baked beans," he said, sidestepping a puddle he suspected wasn't water. "Whole beets. Sliced beets."

"Huh?" a man at the end of the alley said as he stumbled onto the new street. Stanley ignored him.

"Yellow wax beans," he whispered.

"Nic Cage?" the man said, surprised. Stanley glanced at him. He was older than Stanley, but younger than Nic Cage. He looked like a guy who used to play football in highschool but maybe sold cars now. He was smiling and had his phone out, apparently unaware that Nic Cage was wanted for questioning about murders in town.

"I'm going to own this curse," Stanley told him, then swore, trying to clear his head. The man raised his phone to snap a picture and Stanley turned quickly, shielding his face and running into traffic. A Jeep screeched to a halt, narrowly avoiding him as the driver honked and screamed at him.

Stanley kept running, causing cars in the next lane to halt as well. Soon, the road was clogged with angry drivers, honking and yelling. People pointed, recognizing his face.

A couple on the sidewalk were already filming and Stanley stopped, looking around for some means of escape. He stood like a deer in headlights, dead center in the middle of the road. The noise and crowds attracted a bigger crowd. A handful of people grew to a dozen and then two dozen and then even more. The lights of camera flashes filled the street.

"Not the bees," Stanley whispered, panic gripping him tightly. He didn't know what to do.

"Please stop," he said then, finding his own voice once more. "Please leave me alone."

The people either didn't hear or didn't care. He was surrounded now. Honking, pointing, yelling. Cameras filming, faces amused or terrified, likely depending on whether they'd seen the news.

A siren rose above the rest of the noise, steadily growing closer. The police had been called. Someone had ratted out Nic Cage. He had to get away.

"You're drowning," Stanley said, seeing a small break in the crowd near a martini bar. "I'm swimming."

He made a break for it, running as fast as he could. Nic Cage was a better runner than Stanley, it seemed, or at least he felt more confident doing it as Nic Cage. He weaved around cars and then pushed through the crowd, knocking a man down in the process.

"Sorry!" he yelled back, sprinting as fast as Nic Cage's legs would carry him. He wanted to go home, he wanted to hide in his room, but the closer he got to his building, the more he realized it was not an option. If Nic Cage took over, he wouldn't stay put. Worse, Cameron was right there. He didn't trust that he wouldn't hurt his roommate. He couldn't go there. He couldn't go to the clinic, he couldn't go to work. There was no place left that he felt safe.

At the corner of Fourteenth and Woodhurst, he made a right turn and headed towards the park.

It was a terrible idea. The worst idea. And his only idea. The park was where the cops would be looking. They would have to be looking there. But it would be where the other Nic Cages were most likely to show up as well. He'd found them there twice already. Maybe the third time would be the charm. Maybe this time he could get some answers.

His plan was hasty and foolish and made up almost literally on the fly. He ran, his breath coming ragged and heavy, and considered his options. The other Cages would likely be suffering the same condition as him, but they seemed totally out of touch with who they were in the daylight. They were all monster Cages. He was at least still semi-coherent. If he could hold on to that, if he could keep his focus until sunrise, he had a chance.

He needed to capture another Cage. Capture and subdue them. Hold them until the sun rose and then determine who they were and what had happened to them. If he couldn't find the Alpha Cage, he could at least try for Raging Cage and Dog Cage, to see if they knew anything about how they turned and who had done it.

Stanley had no real method of subduing Nic Cage or holding him captive. As it stood, he planned on simply beating whoever he found into unconsciousness and maybe using their own shoelaces to tie them up. He hoped it was one of those "so stupid it has to work" plans he'd heard about in the past. He had the first half down, he just needed to hit the follow through.

In the stories he'd read online, one common theme with werewolves was that their victims would be freed when the wolf that made them was killed. Madame Maleva had told him the same. It was like a chain letter or something. A curse that had a first stop. If the originator was destroyed, then all the cursed down the line were freed. That was why he needed the Alpha Cage. Whoever started the curse had to be the key to ending it. They had to be.

There were police cars parked on the street across from the park as Stanley approached. He stopped running and ducked into the doorway of an apartment building. The two cars were empty, no officers in sight, but they had to be close. Likely in the park, he assumed. Their increased presence would make it harder for him to find what he was looking for. And it also put them at risk. The other Cages had no problem attacking the police, that much was clear.

At some point, if the attacks continued, the police and the Cages would have to have a showdown. Stanley had no idea if a WereCage was immortal or not. Did a silver bullet have to take them out? Could he just walk off a regular bullet? He didn't really want to find out one way or the other.

Stanley crossed the street swiftly but casually enough to not draw attention, his head down as he pretended to text and look as unsuspicious as he could. He breezed into the park, watching everyone and everything he could with his peripheral vision and trying to keep at a normal pace. Just a guy walking in the park, no big deal at all.

He made it to the treeline and then skulked his way to the shadows, doing his best to stay fully out of sight.

The park was alive in a way that seemed different to him. With Nic Cage's senses, and a desire to purposefully remain hidden while looking for signs of others like him, he felt like a wild animal. The air smelled different, felt different on his skin. There was no way the real Nic Cage experienced life like that. It was weird. It was all very weird.

Creeping through the trees, Stanley tried to keep low while listening for any Cageisms or other suspicious sounds. He had to pause and hug a tree trunk for several minutes as a pair of police walking down a path came close and shined a light into the wooded area, nearly catching him. His heart raced, fear gripping him as he was sure they would draw guns and shoot him at any moment. But instead, the beam of light continued on, missing him entirely, and the officers continued on their way.

He made his way towards the pond and the open field on the south side of it, carefully trying to avoid crunching leaves and twigs. Nic Cage was surprisingly light on his feet and it allowed Stanley to move with more stealth than he was used to.

More police were patrolling the path at the pond and Stanley was forced to stop again, crouching low just inside the treeline and looking out over the field and the water.

The officers were engaged in some kind of conversation, though they were too far away for Stanley to make out the words. A third figure was visible as well, not on the pond side but in the field to Stanley's right. It looked to be a man out for a walk , strolling casually through the grass off the path.

For just a moment Stanley dismissed the stranger as a man walking his dog. He could see the leash and the man was in no visible hurry. But as he got closer, his features became easier to distinguish. The hairline that was the same as Stanley's own. The intense stare on his face as his eyes locked onto the police officers approaching from around the edge of the pond. It was Raging Cage. And Stanley had no doubt that, down in the grass, at the end of his leash was Dog Cage.

Stanley was about to yell at the police, to alert them to the presence of the other Cages, when Raging Cage dropped the leash. A furious stream of yelling arose from the grass, bits and pieces of half recognizable quotes from Nicolas Cage movies, before Dog Cage burst from the field, pint-sized and seemingly jet propelled. His tiny legs carried him at a blinding pace towards the officers as Raging Cage closed the gap behind them.

"Take cover, child!" he screamed, leaping into the air. The officers were caught by surprise, as much by the speed of the attack as by the presence of both a tiny Nicolas Cage and a full-sized one assaulting them from a field.

The nearest of the two officers fell without drawing his own weapon. Dog Cage climbed his body like a monkey in pursuit of the most seductive banana in the jungle. The little hands and feet clutched the fabric of his uniform and climbed to the face just as Raging Cage brought his hands down on the man's head like his fists were hammers and the cop's head was a mole in need of dramatic whacking.

Dog Cage growled and bit at the officer's face, causing the man to scream while he fell. The second officer drew his gun and ordered them off, taking aim at the larger of the two.

"Hands where I can see them now," the still-standing officer ordered.

"My daddy once said 'if you don't make a choice, the choice makes you,'" Raging Cage said. He turned on the armed officer and lunged. Two shots rang out, hitting Cage point blank in the chest. He fell in a heap while Dog Cage cried out in surprise. The little Cage turned on the second officer and another shot echoed through the park.

Stanley could see the hole open in Dog Cage's face, the bullet hitting him square in the forehead. He covered his own mouth, smothering a cry of shock before he gave himself away.

The uninjured officer went to check on his partner while the two Cages lay motionless where they had fallen. Stanley had no idea if they were dead, but they certainly looked the part.

Along the path to Stanley's other side, a new figure appeared. This one was in no hurry but instead seemed to just be taking in the scene. And, once again, the gait, the body shape, and the hairline were all too familiar. A third Cage. Maybe Bitey, the one who had turned him initially, or even Alpha Cage. Or someone new altogether. The trouble with identifying different Nic Cages was the fact they all looked like Nic Cage.

Raging Cage stirred, getting to his feet with a sudden fierceness. The officer had radioed for backup but had turned his back on the fallen Cages. Raging Cage capitalized and set upon him as well. The officer screamed as Cage's teeth sank into his ear and pulled it away from his head with a spray of dark blood.

Stanley grimaced, looking from the attack back to the third Cage. The newcomer was not approaching, only watching the scene play out. Maybe he was willing to let the others finish the police off, or maybe he was waiting for backup to arrive. That would end with more dead. Or more Nic Cages. Stanley couldn't allow it.

He ran from the trees, heading towards the third Cage. His doppelgänger spotted him immediately but made no move to flee or even show signs of fear or trepidation. Nic Cage's smiling face simply locked eyes with him and waited for his approach.

"You've been around a lot of corpses. Is that normal?" Cage asked, pointing to the officer fighting with Raging Cage. The urge to reply with a quote from *The Rock* was powerful, but Stanley resisted.

"Who are you?" he demanded. The other Cage's eyes narrowed, and he looked at Stanley with suspicion.

"On any other day, that might seem strange."

"Talk to me," Stanley insisted. "The real you. Not Nic Cage."

The other Cage grinned then. He was wearing a suit, dress shoes with no socks, and a gold chain around his neck. He looked like he was a sleazeball from a club, trying to pick up women far too young for him. He was Cage as a villain.

"I'll kill all of you. To the break of dawn. To the break of dawn, baby," Cage told him.

"Are you the one that bit me? Who bit you?" Stanley asked, trying to sound authoritative and angry. "How did this all start?"

"Plan B. Why don't we just kill each other?" Cage replied, his smile growing wider.

Stanley felt a surge of panic, though nothing had even happened yet. Then Cage moved, a blur of motion and manic yelling as he came at Stanley with his fingers curved like claws and his teeth bared like fangs.

Cage took him to the ground, biting at the air around his face. Eyes wide and titters of laughter escaping his gaping rictus, he snarled like a beast and tried to pull at Stanley's clothes even as he leaned in to try to bite his cheeks and nose.

Stanley had never truly been in a fight in his life. Once, in middle school, a kid named Bobby Fulcher punched him right in the nose for no reason he was ever made aware of. It bled like his face was a fountain and he had to go home and change his shirt. That was the most violent thing he had ever experienced, and he hadn't even lifted his hands during it. He had no idea how to fight.

His hands wrapped around Nic Cage's throat and he pushed as hard as he could, holding the snapping jaws at bay. He was hoping his double would at least try to grab him by the wrists, but he did not. He kept grabbing at Stanley's shirt and face, punching and clawing and slapping whatever he could like some kind of deranged, sugar-addled toddler.

Stanley squeezed Cage's throat, desperate to make the man back off and leave him alone. He wasn't trying to kill him, but he wasn't about to let the man kill him, either. Cage retched and choked and sputtered a half-realized quote that Stanley didn't even recognize.

"Just tell me how this happened," he demanded through clenched teeth, holding Cage at arm's length.

Instead of an answer, a gunshot reverberated through the night. Stanley was certain he heard it whiz past his head and let out a quiet scream when he realized what was happening. More police officers had arrived and one had tried to shoot him, or the Cage on top of him. To their eyes it wouldn't have made a difference, it was two of the same guy wrestling on a path in the park.

He released Cage, fear and adrenaline making him feel like his entire body was made of electricity. Cage laughed, staring wide eyed down at Stanley.

"What's in the bag?" Cage croaked before leaning in too close to his face. "A shark or something?"

Another shot rang out and grazed Cage's arm. The man yelped and got to his feet, turning and running for the trees. Stanley scrambled to do the same as two new police officers rushed towards them, shouting orders to not move.

One of the officers fired another round at Cage, and Stanley took off after his double. He ran as fast as Nic Cage's legs would carry him, pushing himself as hard as he possibly could. Another shot followed, and another. He couldn't tell if they were shooting at him or Cage or both. He wasn't going to stop or look back. He needed to run.

Sirens surrounded the park, and Stanley could see lights cutting through trees and across fields. More police were closing in on multiple sides. They were coming to aid their fallen comrade, and chase down Cage, and himself as well. They were spreading themselves thin in all the confusion.

The other Cage was as fast as Stanley, if not faster, and seemed to run with no fear of being seen or plan to escape. He stormed through the trees and out of the park onto the street, right into another pair of police officers, catching them both by surprise.

He slammed the head of one officer into the door of his own car and then dragged the other to the ground, moving less like a human and more like an animal. The officer screamed as Cage positioned his thumbs over the man's eyes. Before he could plunge them in, Stanley tackled him again, taking the opportunity to grab him by the lapels and bounce his head off the curb.

"Why do you care about these people?" Cage asked. "They don't care about you. None of them."

Stanley wasn't sure if it was a quote or not, but had no time to ponder the point. Cage punched him in the nose, just like Bobby Fulcher had. He cried out in pain as his vision blurred briefly. Cage knocked him aside and got up again, running into the street and causing a car to swerve and crash into the parked police cruiser.

"Move and you're dead!" a cop yelled from the park. Stanley swore and ignored the man, scrambling to his feet and hitting the street in pursuit of Cage once more. A bullet hit the police car behind him and he nearly fell.

Brakes squealed, and he looked up in time to see the front grille of an old Pontiac just before it planted a two ton steel kiss on his face. He flew back into the street and landed with a grunt, pain searing down his body like he had been hit by lightning and then, just as quickly, sliding away again.

Nic Cage's body was strong. The pain was real, but it was short-lived. He rolled over, gulping air, and got to his feet again. He couldn't let the other man get away. Not for anything, not even a Pontiac.

Cage had reached the other side of the road and was pushing pedestrians out of his way. A crowd of people attracted by the commotion had formed once more, phones at the ready to try to capture the next viral video.

Stanley reached the sidewalk, shaken but recovering much faster than he should have, just as Cage grabbed a man filming the chase with an iPhone and lifted him bodily from the ground. He swung the man towards Stanley as though he were a sack of potatoes.

The man screamed as he hit a different stranger on the sidewalk and they both collapsed in a painful heap. People yelled and shouted, some in confusion, others in anger or fear. The scene, Nic Cage chasing Nic Cage with a garnish of police gunfire, had to be hard to wrap heads around. The only reason Stanley wasn't panicking alongside them was that he hadn't given himself time to do so. He needed to catch Cage and make him talk, even if that meant holding him captive until sunrise.

Cage reached the end of the block, pushing people to the ground and tossing others back towards Stanley to try to slow his progress. In Nic Cage's body, Stanley was nimble and fast, however. He jumped over the fallen pedestrians and weaved through those left standing, pacing Cage as well as he could and staying only a few yards behind.

They reached a busy intersection, and Cage didn't hesitate at all. He burst into the flow of traffic, causing cars to honk and swerve. An SUV nearly ran into him and he jumped onto the hood of a Nissan to escape it, running across the still moving vehicle before leaping into the next lane and causing a pickup truck to brake and get rear-ended by a bus.

"You are a vicious snowflake!" Cage yelled with a laugh as the truck was pushed forward. Stanley had to move quickly, ducking back to the sidewalk he had just left to avoid being hit. Cage escaped into the crowd of onlookers on the other side of the street while three more cars joined the pile up caused by the bus crash.

Police were already running from the park, and Stanley had no time to pause and consider a plan. He had to go.

Cage had already vanished, capitalizing on the accident. Flashes illuminated the night as people snapped photo after photo of Stanley, others just filming and yelling at him. He ran again, heading up the street, away from the park and the crashed cars.

More police cars converged on the scene. Stanley had no idea there were even so many cops in town. He heard the sirens and saw the lights and cut through an alley, heading one street over to try to escape notice.

He erupted from the alley and dodged a couple carrying a bag of leftovers from a restaurant. In the back of his mind, he cursed himself for missing his dinner with Sara. Surely she'd understand. He had no doubt footage of what happened would be on the news in no time. Just an average, everyday Nic Cage park chase.

A police car raced up the street and he cursed out loud this time, drawing looks from other passersby. He ran to the next alley he could see and leapt up onto a dumpster beside a dollar store, then grabbed the bottom rung of a fire escape.

Stanley had never been known for his upper body strength and, truth be told, had never actually used or even thought the words "upper body strength" in his life that he could recall. But Nic Cage had upper body strength. He pulled himself up and raced up the ladder to the roof of the shop.

There was a massive air conditioning unit and a few beer cans on top of the building, but little else. He ran to the edge and looked across at the next building, which had an equally empty rooftop. More sirens filled the street, and he could see the flashes of red and blue lights across the storefronts and apartments on the far side of the road. If he walked to the edge of the building and looked down, he was sure there would be at least four squad cars there. Someone had seen him climb up. They'd be on him in no time.

Though he was not much of a spiritual man, Stanley said a little prayer as he headed to the far side of the roof and then turned around. He took a deep breath and then broke into a flat run. He was getting used to being Nic Cage, used to the way the body felt and what it could do. He reached the edge of the roof and then jumped.

The feeling of flight was brief but remarkable. He sailed from one rooftop to the next and landed as though he did this sort of thing all the time. He couldn't hold back the laugh as he continued onward. He leaped from rooftop to rooftop, keeping to the back side of the buildings so no one on the streets would be able to see him.

Soon enough, he'd reach the final roof on the block and the flashing lights of police cars were more than half a block behind him. He raced down the fire escape to the back of the building and crossed to the next street, further distancing himself from his pursuers.

Once out of sight of the police, he took his button down shirt off once more and retrieved his phone. Just a guy with his head down, reading text messages. He casually walked up another block and crossed over again. No one noticed him now, or they didn't give any sign of it.

It took everything Stanley had in him to stay calm and try to be normal. Normal pace, normal behavior. No running. It took him fifteen minutes to circle back to his apartment and make his way back up the fire escape, where no one would notice him.

He crept into his room and then sat on the floor right below the window. The room was dark, and he had been quiet enough that Cameron had no idea he'd returned. Out in the night sirens still blared, but they were distant now. They were searching far from him. Maybe they weren't searching for him at all anymore. Maybe the other Cage had caught their attention once more.

Enough police had seen him, seen them, that he knew they'd have a serious problem. Three full sized Nic Cages and one pint-sized one. There was no way to explain it. And it had rattled the police something fierce. Stanley wasn't one hundred percent sure of proper police procedures, but he felt like the number of bullets they squeezed off with little care for where they were going had to be against the rules. The cops were looking to kill him. Looking to kill all the Cages, likely for what they had done to the other officers the night before. And now another officer was down, though he had no idea how badly injured. Dog Cage had bitten him, though. If he wasn't dead, he'd be prowling the park like the rest of them in twenty-four hours' time. Things just kept getting worse.

Tentatively, Stanley touched his own face. Or, rather, Nic Cage's face. He'd taken a Pontiac right in the chops and he seemed fine. He didn't even feel bruised. Were the Cages immortal? That could really compound problems. Maybe he'd have to resort to silver bullets if he wanted to end the curse. But that would mean killing someone. He'd only just been in his first real fight, escalating to killing seemed like a big step. He also didn't own any silver aside from his necklace, and that seemed much too small to make a bullet out of.

"I don't know what I believe anymore," Stanley muttered as he got slowly to his feet. He shook his head then. Those words were not his. That was Cage talking, he realized. All the adrenaline had seeped from his veins and he was feeling exhausted. The Nic Cage in his mind was pushing its will onto him and it was becoming harder to resist.

He needed to find some way to hold himself in his own room, to keep himself locked up or restrained until morning, but he had nothing. The best he could think of was using some old paracord he had in the closet that he'd used on a camping trip years ago.

Stanley opened the closet and began rifling through boxes on the top shelf. He had used it to secure a sleeping bag. He was sure he had nearly a whole roll of it in there somewhere.

A box fell to the ground with a thud as he began searching more recklessly, knocking things aside in a more desperate bid to find what he was looking for.

"Stan?" Cameron called from out in the apartment.

"Today is the first day of the rest of my life," he called back. No. That wasn't what he wanted to say. That was more Cage.

"Okay?" Cameron replied. There was a pause, and Stanley threw another box on the ground. The lid opened, and the paracord was inside. Stanley very nearly clapped as he crouched down and retrieved it.

"Do you think you're Nic Cage right now?" Cameron asked then. Stanley winced, unrolling the length of blue and white rope.

"I'm the guy you yelled at this morning," he answered, tying one end of the rope around his ankle and securing it with a series of knots.

"What?"

"Nothing," he shot back, struggling to not let Cage answer again. "Gonna sleep now, night night."

He looped the rope around his other ankle and then took the loose end and began winding it around his bed frame. He could feel Nic Cage poking at the corners of his consciousness, getting closer and closer to usurping his own and taking over. He couldn't risk being out on the street again, not with that face. And he couldn't risk putting Cameron in danger.

He pulled the ropes as tight as he could, running a pair of loops around his wrists and then using his mouth to cinch it tight when he was finished. The result was him in Nic Cage's body, doubled up on the floor next to the bed, incapable of doing much of anything. If he had more time to consider his options, he might have done it in a more comfortable position. He'd remember that for next time.

## Chapter Ten

Sunlight, exhaust and the sounds of traffic woke Stanley like a slap in the face. He sat up in his bed, a sour taste in his mouth, and turned his head to the source of the disturbance that had awoken him. His bedroom window was wide open, and the city outside had not been gracious enough to let him sleep in.

Memories of the previous night seemed to spill over one another in his head, and he looked around the room. The paracord rope was piled in front of his bathroom door. He had untied himself at some point and then... gone to bed?

His gaze turned to the bedroom door. Cameron had been awake. And talking to him.

He got out of bed quickly and then grimaced when he saw that he was naked. His clothes were strewn about the room, as though Cage had been angry at being dressed at all. He grabbed a pair of sweatpants and slipped into them quickly as he made for the bedroom door.

"Cameron?" he called out, opening the door. "Cam!"

The apartment smelled like coffee and Pop Tarts. Cameron sat at the kitchen island, reading something on his laptop and drinking a coffee. The Pop Tarts had already been eaten.

"Hey buddy. Weird night, right?"

"What?" Stanley asked. Cameron got up and went to the cupboard to retrieve a mug.

"It was not what I was expecting. I don't know what to think anymore."

"Cameron, what the hell happened?" he asked. His roommate put the mug on the island and poured a second coffee.

"Your little friend didn't tell you?" Cameron teased. Stanley raised an eyebrow. The apartment did not look in disarray at all. And Cameron appeared to be uninjured. Maybe he'd just untied himself and gone to sleep.

"Tell me what, Cam?"

"We hung out. It was cool. It wasn't a big deal. You don't need to act weird about it"

"You hung out?" Stanley asked. Cameron nodded, pushing the mug towards Stanley.

"Oh yeah, it was a hoot. We watched *Con Air*, and he said every single line, at the exact right moment, with the exact right inflection."

"He did not."

"He did! And then he gave me a ton of behind the scenes information. He told me that, during production, he could only eat hard boiled eggs and whole milk," Cameron said. Stanley made a face.

"That can't be true."

"I have no idea, but he sounded very sure. And why didn't you ever tell me that Nic Cage's character was named Cameron in that movie? That's fun. What a fun thing to know. I like Nic Cage."

"Are you seriously okay?" Stanley asked. Cameron shrugged, taking another sip of his coffee.

"I could kill a breakfast burrito but that aside, I feel fine. You, however, seem unwell this morning."

"I just don't get it. Nothing happened? You just watched movies?"

Cameron smiled and rolled his eyes over the edge of his coffee mug as he had another sip.

"You sound like a jealous boyfriend, Stan. What exactly do you think I did with Nic Cage last night?"

"Oh. Oh, God, no. That's not what I meant," Stanley said, suddenly picking up on the lascivious undertones of what Cameron was saying. "I just meant you're okay. Cage didn't go crazy or... wait, you didn't sleep with Nic Cage, did you?"

"Did you? Last I saw, he was headed back to your room."

"Well, obviously, it's my room."

"He didn't have to go, I mean... huh." Cameron stopped what he was saying mid-thought, staring at Stanley.

"What?" Stan asked.

"He had that mark on his neck, too. The bite," Cameron told him, pointing to the bite mark that Stan got from the original Nic Cage. "Like exactly the same."

His eyes drifted from the bite to Stan's eyes, and he could see the realization dawning on his roommate. All that time, he'd still been doubting Stanley. He'd apparently even thought Stan had brought actual Nic Cage home with him and the two of them had watched movies while Stanley slept.

They stared at each other for a moment in pure silence, Stanley allowing Cameron to finally adjust to what he must have told him a dozen times by now.

"Oh my God, you're Nic Cage!"

"I'm a WereCage," Stanley corrected. Cameron clicked his tongue and made a face.

"Maybe don't say that word to people. But oh my God, you're not crazy. This is real. That really happened!"

"We've been over this," Stanley pointed out.

"I was drinking, Stanley, please give me a moment."

Cameron crossed the room and extended a finger, poking Stanley in the chest.

"What are you doing?"

"Making sure you're not like Silly Putty or something," Cameron stated.

"What?"

"I don't know! I'm trying not to freak out. You turned into Nic Cage!"

"I know. And there are other ones. And one tried to kill me last night, and another one killed a cop again. It's getting out of hand, Cam."

"That is not in hand," Cameron agreed. He finished his coffee and sat down, tapping his foot nervously while he took Stanley's coffee and began to drink it as well.

"Did you hear anything on the news this morning?" he asked, trying to distract Cameron. His roommate scoffed.

"I'm not my Opa, Stanley. I don't watch the news."

"Well check. I need to know what happened in the park," Stanley insisted.

Cameron opened a new window on his laptop and brought up a page of local news. A shaky video of Nic Cage chasing Nic Cage through traffic loaded with the story and started to auto-play.

"Oh damn, did you know there's two of you?"

"I told you that already! Dog Cage! And Raging Cage!"

"Which one is this?" Cameron asked, his eyes glued to the screen. It was as if spending the night watching *Con Air* had flipped some kind of switch inside of him. One that made him believe Stanley but also made him forget everything Stanley had already told him.

"I think the cops killed Raging Cage, but maybe not. I got hit by a car last night and I feel fine. I don't think we can die."

Cameron tore his eyes away from the video and his dumbfounded expression fell on Stanley.

"You got hit by a car? And you're immortal? Stanley, what the hell?"

"I don't know if I'm immortal. But I shook off the car hit pretty easily. And this other Cage picked up a man and threw him at me. A whole man."

"A whole man?" Cameron clarified.

"A whole man," Stanley confirmed.

"Is Nic Cage that strong normally?"

"Cameron, I think we need to accept the possibility that what is happening is not normal Nic Cagery at all."

Cameron returned to the video in time to see the bus slam into the pickup truck and the other Cage vanish into the night. Whoever was filming turned to Stanley as Nic Cage then and caught a few seconds of his panicked expression before he finally fled the scene as well.

"Oh God, Stan," Cameron said quietly. His eyes scanned the page. Stanley tried to read the article over his shoulder as he scrolled down the page but only saw headlines about missing persons and exclusive Nic Cage video.

"What?" he asked.

"The attack left three dead, including police officer Antonio Gates. A warrant had previously been issued for the arrest of Cage, but representatives for the actor claim he has been in Bulgaria shooting a film which officials and witness accounts confirm. When asked if police are considering this the work of perpetrators wearing disguises, Chief Santoro had no comment," Cameron read out loud. He looked back at Stanley then.

"Three people last night and two the night before," he told him. Stanley looked back at the computer screen.

"What about injuries? Survivors? Anyone who was bitten?"

Cameron scrolled through the document to the end and shook his head.

"Says several bystanders were taken to hospital with non-life threatening injuries, but it doesn't say what they were."

Stanley cursed. That could have been people pushed to the ground who sprained an ankle or it could have been ones with giant Nic Cage bites in their asses.

"You need to do something, Stanley."

Stanley made a frustrated sound in lieu of swearing.

"I know that, Cameron. What do you think I've been trying to do? Did you really think I was lying this whole time? After everything I told you? You even told me to call the cops before! You never believed any of it?"

Cameron looked offended but also ashamed as he briefly cast his eyes away.

"It was a lot, Stan. Okay? It was a lot. I thought maybe it was in your head. Maybe if I humored you or, like, I don't know. Like I get mental illness, you know? I get that. I can help with that. But I don't get this. This isn't supposed to be real." He gestured vaguely and furtively in Stanley's general direction as he said "this," an unclear attempt to cover everything relating to Stanley's condition.

"Well no shit, Cam. I'm the one who turns into Nic Cage. How do you think I feel?"

Cameron closed his eyes and took a long, deep breath.

"Okay," he said, eyes still closed. "Okay, this is a moment."

He opened his eyes, and the two men looked at each other.

"I'm sorry I didn't believe you, Stanley."

"It's fine. I get it. It's literally the dumbest thing I've ever heard. Or it would be if people weren't dying."

"Right. So we're saying this works like werewolfery? You get bit and you turn?"

"Werewolfery?" Stanley asked. Cameron shrugged.

"Stanley, I'm not a veterinarian."

"Lycanthropy. It doesn't matter. Yeah, that's what happens, I think. You get bit and you turn."

"So there are at least four of you. But we're going to say you're safe because you don't seem to bite people. Right?"

"Right," he agreed, slightly offended by Cameron's tone.

"So at least three. But who knows how many more after last night? If all three bit someone yesterday, there will be six tonight. Then twelve tomorrow. Then twenty-four. That's like six billion people in a month. That's it. That's the end of the world."

"Wilford Brimley," Stanley agreed.

"Wilford Goddamn Brimley."

"Wait, one month? Brimley said three years in *The Thing*," Stanley pointed out.

"He's a son of a bitch," Cameron said by way of an explanation. Stanley ran a hand through his air, taking a series of deep breaths to try to calm himself. Three years was too soon. A month was so much worse.

"It's not an exact science," Cameron added then.

"What, math? It's the most exact science," Stanley pointed out. His roommate shrugged.

"I mean, there have to be hiccups. Crossing oceans. People who hide. I'm sure humanity has more than a month."

"Two months?" Stanley asked.

"Maybe more. Maybe a lot more. It's just three today. There's time to stop it."

Stanley wanted to believe that. He needed to. But convincing himself was not going well. The police had no idea what they were doing. They were in well over their heads. They were looking for actual Nic Cage in Bulgaria when they had video footage, from in town, of at least two Nic Cages.

People would react just like Cameron. Stanley could see that now. They would not want to believe the truth because the truth was an absurdity. The truth was a Nic Cage movie writ large across reality, complete with screaming and Nic Cage noises. They would resist accepting reality until the last possible moment, when it was far too late. When Nic Cage's manic jaws were already closing over their throats.

While police and officials tried to figure out why Nic Cage was in Bulgaria and people in town were being killed by him, the other Cages would continue their attacks. New Cages would join them. Murder and mayhem would increase just like Cameron and Wilford Brimley had predicted.

"How do we stop it?" Cameron asked.

"I have an idea," Stanley replied. His only idea. An idea based on the words of a back alley psychic and Google. It was like trying to build an airplane out of scrap metal after watching an episode of *MacGyver*. There was no reason to suspect it would work. But it was all they had to go on.

"If you kill the first one, the source of the curse, then it releases all the others. That's what I've been trying to do. To find Bitey Cage."

"Bitey. Heh," Cameron interrupted. Stanley continued.

"I think the other guy in that video was him, the one that caused the bus accident. But I don't know. I lost him last night. I have to find him today. I have to end this."

"That guy seems psychotic," his roommate pointed out. "You're going to need to be armed with something."

"That's the thing. I don't think anything hurts us when we're Nic Cage."

"Silver bullets," Cam suggested. "That works in every movie."

"I don't have any silver. Or a gun. And if I had a gun, I'm pretty sure I'd shoot myself or like a cabbie or something."

"That's a solid point," Cameron agreed. "But you do have silver. You can use that necklace you always wear. And my mom gave me a box of all my grandma's old jewelry after she died instead of, you know, anything useful. It's useful now!"

"I can't whip him with a silver chain," Stanley pointed out. Cameron scoffed and got out of his seat.

"Just give me a second. I have an idea."

He retreated to his room while Stanley remained in the kitchen. He stared at the article on the laptop screen, the frozen image of Nic Cage's panicked face, Stanley's face, in fact. He had been so close. He had his hands on Bitey Cage. And he let him get away.

The fact that he had no idea if Bitey and Alpha were the same was a frustration he couldn't put into words. But Bitey at least predated Stanley, so that meant he was closer to the source. If he wasn't the Alpha, he may have been attacked by the Alpha. In the light of day, he'd know what Stanley wanted to know. Where the attack happened and when.

He wondered what the others were doing now that they were back to themselves. Raging Cage, if he was still alive, and Bitey. When they were back to normal, did they remember anything of what had happened? Stanley could not remember his time as Cage, not when Nic took over completely. But his Cage was still not violent. There had to be a reason for it.

In the light of day, even if the others couldn't remember their own actions, they had to know something had happened. They knew that they too had been attacked by Nic Cage at some point. They knew they were waking up in strange places, just as Stanley had done. He wondered if they were as frightened and confused as he was.

"Who needs a gun when you have blood sports, right?" Cameron asked, returning to the room. He held an aluminum baseball bat in one hand and a jumble of silver jewelry in the other.

"That bat's aluminum," Stanley pointed out. Cameron rolled his eyes.

"Obviously. But it doesn't matter." He set the bat down and began linking a handful of chains together.

"Give me yours," he said to Stanley.

"Why?"

"Because I'm starting an all male review called the Chain Gang and I need costumes. Just give me the damn chain," he insisted. Stanley frowned and took the chain off, handing it to his friend. Cameron hooked one end to some of his more delicate silver chains and then hooked another one to that. He managed to weave six of them together and then began wrapping the extensive length around the end of the baseball bat.

"Oh," Stanley said, finally understanding what his roommate was up to. Once the chains were in place, he forced a handful of earrings with the posts out through the chain as well, creating a makeshift silver barbed-wire baseball bat. He handed it to Stanley.

"Now you have a werewolf killer."

"WereCage," Stanley corrected.

"Really not liking that word," Cam told him.

Stanley lifted the bat. The chains looked secure, though he was afraid the whole thing might break to pieces after a single hit. Cameron's grandmother's jewelry did not look like it had been designed for melee combat. But maybe one hit would be all that he needed. One solid blow to Alpha Cage's head might knock the therianthropy right out of him and free up everyone else cursed with it.

"You'll have to think of a way to walk around with it that doesn't make you look like a maniac," Cameron added. Stanley nodded. It would draw attention to him, he was sure. Especially using it after nightfall as Nic Cage.

"I wish there was something I could do during the day to end this. Something as myself," Stanley stated.

"I'd get my affairs in order," his roommate suggested.

"What?"

"Just saying. The cops are going to be out for blood. One Nic Cage will probably be as good as another to them. You're going to have to be careful tonight. Every night, I guess. Until this is all over. However that might be."

"I'm going to figure this out," Stanley assured him. He had to now because there was no one else in the world who seemed capable of doing so. It would take a super powered, maybe immortal Nic Cage to take out another super powered, maybe immortal Nic Cage.

"I don't have affairs to even get in order. I have nothing."

"You could write a will," Cam suggested. Stanley chuckled dryly.

"If I die, you can have the four hundred dollars in my account and whatever you want from my room."

"Thanks, Stan. That means a lot," Cameron replied. Stanley hadn't meant it as a genuine, caring offer. It didn't matter, though. He could try to call his mother, though she often seemed to ignore his calls and let them go to voicemail. Not that he called often, either. It had been a while.

Stanley's eyes widened then. He had to call Sara. He had stood her up the night before and had completely forgotten about their dinner.

"Crap," he said out loud.

"Nurse Sara?" Cameron guessed. Stanley rushed back to his room in search of his phone.

## Chapter Eleven

Stanley grabbed his pants from where Nic Cage had tossed them in a heap and pulled out his cell phone. There were no missed calls or texts at all. He was surprised that Sara hadn't tried to contact him. But she made it clear she thought he'd be crazy to stand her up the day before.

He called her and the phone rang just twice before voicemail picked up. He called again and went to voicemail once more.

"Hello, Sara. This is Stanley from the date we sorta didn't have last night. I swear it wasn't my fault. There was what you might call an incident yesterday? Um... yeah. No. But yeah, if we can talk, you'll see I'm not insane. It's for real. My roommate can even tell you. This sounds lame, but I'm really sorry and I hope I can talk to you soon."

He hung up the phone and stared at it for a moment. He thought about sending her a text message, but he was afraid maybe she'd already blocked his number. Everything could have been ruined already, all because of Nic Cage.

If the world was going to end, maybe in less than a month, he was not going to take it sitting down. He had to at least try his best. He had to let Sara know that he wasn't the kind of jerk who would just stand her up. If not now, then he might never get the chance again.

Stanley got dressed quickly. He could plot out his evening later on, how he would find Bitey Cage and maybe beat the devil out of him with the silver studded bat. But first, he needed to find Sara. He needed to get to the clinic.

He left his room. Cameron was still at the kitchen island with another cup of coffee.

"That was fast," he said. Stanley shook his head.

"She didn't answer. I need to go to the clinic and talk to her, explain what happened."

"You can't do that," Cameron told him.

"Why not?"

"You can't tell her you turned into Nic Cage and fought another Nic Cage."

"I told her that days ago. I told you that days ago," Stanley pointed out. Cameron shook his head.

"Yeah, but that's when we thought you were mentally unwell. This is real. This absolutely has to be kept on the down low."

"She has to know. I like her. And the world is going to end in thirty days."

"The city will be gone in a couple of weeks, if we're being technical," Cameron interrupted.

"Come on," Stanley said, feeling a twinge in his gut like he might be sick.

"Sorry. Just saying."

"Great, sure. Our world is over in a couple of weeks. I want to die happy if I have to die."

"But you should really try to kill that first one and end the curse. Save the world. If you can," Cameron told him, nodding to the baseball bat.

"I will. But I can't do that right now, so I'm going to talk to Sara. I owe her that. She was the first one who believed me. The only one, it turns out."

"I believe you now," Cameron pointed out defensively.

"I need to do this. I'll be back before the sun goes down," Stanley told him, heading for the door. Cameron frowned and clicked something on his computer.

"Hey Stan, what's with the werewolfery and the moon, anyway? Full moon was two days ago. Aren't you free and clear now?"

"I thought so. But it happened last night, anyway. If it doesn't happen tonight, then great, but I'm not betting on it."

"Weird. Well, make good choices," his roommate said.

Stanley was not sure how to reply, so he simply nodded and left. He had no idea how he'd managed to get so far in life while having nothing at all to show for it. Cam had told him to get his affairs in order and they already were because he had no affairs to speak of. He had coasted into nothingness. He was like a fart in a windstorm, inconsequential and leaving no mark on the world whatsoever. If he dropped down in the lobby, the only one who would notice would be Cam when he didn't pay rent.

And now the fate of the world was on his shoulders. On his stolen Nic Cage shoulders.

Stanley had never wanted to be a big deal. He never dreamed of being a star athlete when he was a kid, owing in no small part to the fact he could barely play any sport. He never planned to cure cancer or built a rocket because he wasn't smart enough for either. He wouldn't solve crimes or fight fires because he didn't have the motivation, the drive or the strength. He'd never had a real goal he could think of. How the hell had he missed that boat?

It sucked that the thing kicking him in the ass was a full body paranormal transformation into his favorite actor combined with an associated apocalypse. He would have preferred maybe just a moment of zen and self-actualization. Whatever it was that convinced other people to get their heads on straight.

He made his way to the walk-in clinic, running over what he might say to Sara in his head. He wanted to be honest, but he didn't want to sound like a walking red flag. She already knew about the Nic Cage bite and was okay with it, so he wanted to believe she'd be understanding about what happened.

Stanley wasn't sure how one broke the news to a girl that they had turned into Nic Cage outside of the restaurant and then fought another Nic Cage while police tried to kill them both. He could just say that, he supposed. Just lay it out like that and see what she thought. He didn't want to be forgiven for missing dinner. He just wanted her to know why it happened. And maybe salvage a second chance.

He opened the door to the clinic when he got there, taking a calming breath before walking in, and then paused right inside the door. The nurse at the front desk was a man with a square head and a well-trimmed goatee. The two of them made eye contact, and Stanley scowled unintentionally. The nurse noticed and looked unamused.

"Can I help you?" the man asked.

"I was looking for Nurse Wayland. Is she not… here?"

"It's her day off and also this is a medical clinic, not a coffee shop," the man informed him.

"I don't want a coffee," Stanley said. The nurse sighed loudly.

"It's not a speakeasy. You can't come here to socialize."

"A speakeasy? How old are you?" he asked. The nurse looked to be in his thirties. Maybe he was raised by a grandparent.

"Do you need to see a doctor, sir?"

"Not today, no," Stan told him. He turned and left the clinic before the nurse could share another quip with him. She wasn't answering his calls and wasn't at work. He'd hit a dead end.

The idea to try to Google her came to mind, but he quickly talked himself out of it. He didn't want to be a creep, and that seemed like a serious creep move. He would just have to wait for her to want to contact him. And if it never happened again…

Stanley sighed. If he never spoke to her again, then that was what would happen. He didn't like it, but he had other things he needed to worry about as well. The least he could do was try to save the world so she could have the time to decide whether she wanted to see him again.

He decided to return home. There was no need to visit any psychics today, and he was definitely not returning to the park. He needed to plan how to take out Bitey Cage when he found him. The silver studded bat was a great start, but he'd need to do more.

Cameron had not moved by the time Stanley returned home. His roommate grimaced as Stanley entered.

"This bodes poorly," he stated. Stanley tossed his keys on the kitchen island.

"She's not working today. Won't take my calls, either. I think I may have blown it."

"Ghosting a first date is never a good idea,' Cameron agreed. "Especially for a guy like you."

"What do you mean, a guy like me?" he asked. His roommate fixed him with an unimpressed stare and then waved the question away.

"So what now? You're not going to work, are you? That would be so depressing. Like a full body embrace of ennui."

"No, I'm not. I have to make a plan for tonight. We have to try to trap Bitey Cage. If he's not the Alpha, then beating his head in with a bat won't do much good."

Cameron considered that for a moment, and then finally nodded his agreement.

"This is true. You don't want your first murder to be pointless."

"It's not murder! I'm not murdering anyone," Stanley clarified. The other Cages were murdering people. He was doing what he was doing to help people.

"Don't feel bad. I'm not calling you a murderer. I'm just saying that, to fix this problem, you need to, you know, murder."

"Stop saying murder!" Stanley pleaded. Cameron raised his hands defensively.

"Yes, fine, alright. Aggressively kill."

"It's not… I'm trying to save people's lives. From a monster."

"Right. Agreed," Cameron said, nodding emphatically. Stanley could see he was itching to say it again. But it wasn't murder. It was necessary. Like killing a rabid animal. It wasn't malicious. It was for the good of everyone.

"If there's a way we can trap him somehow, that's what we need to do," Stanley said. Cameron continued nodding, a thoughtful look on his face.

"I noticed you've started saying 'we' a lot. Is that a conscious decision on your part?"

"Come on, Cam. Help me with this. We need ideas. How to trap Nic Cage."

"Super powered, maybe immortal Nic Cage," Cameron clarified. Stanley nodded.

"Yeah. Do you know anything about trapping? Or snares?"

Cameron made a face while Stanley started making himself a coffee.

"We've met before, right?" he asked Stanley. "When have I shown aptitude for trapping?"

"You're smart. Well-read. I don't know."

"Yes, I am. But no, I don't. You'll need to ponder a new solution. But maybe try a disguise this time. Not just to trick Nic Cage, but the police as well. You can't walk around with that man's face right now."

"That's a good idea," Stanley agreed, adding sugar to his cup. "Maybe sunglasses and a hat? Or a hoodie?"

"Very James Bond," Cameron said. "Whatever makes you fade into the background. You don't want to get shot."

"No. No, I don't," he agreed. Getting shot was quite far down his list of wants.

He drank his coffee while he tried to craft a plan for trapping Bitey Cage. He had never trapped anything before and wasn't sure Cage would be likely to fall for anything he could come up with. But he did have one thing going for him. He was also Nic Cage. Super powered, maybe immortal Nic Cage. He didn't necessarily need to set a trap. He could be the trap himself. He could use the paracord and just tie the other Cage up and drag him back home. He'd just do a better job than he did on himself. It'd be easier with the full use of his hands.

"You know, when you were out, I was thinking about why this is happening, even when it's not a full moon," Cameron told him.

"You found something online?"

"God no. The internet is useless for stuff like this. But what if you're just *Moonstruck*?"

There was a moment of silence between them, and Stanley waited for some kind of followup. When it was clear there was none, he was forced to reply.

"I don't know what that's supposed to mean."

"*Moonstruck*, man!" Cameron said, holding up his hands in a theatrical manner.

"I, no. No, I still don't know what that means."

"It's a Nic Cage movie. *Moonstruck*. With Cher, you know?"

"No, yeah, no. I get that part. But what are you trying to tell me here?"

"It's *Moonstruck*! You turn into Nic Cage at night even when the moon isn't full. Because you're *Moonstruck*. Because it's Nic Cage. Don't make me draw a goddamn picture."

"I have no idea -"

"Stop!" Cameron insisted. "You quote his movies. You slip in and out of characters, right? All the other ones do, too?"

"Yeah, it's a whole weird thing."

"Exactly. So what if all of you are *Moonstruck* Cages? Don't say it doesn't make sense. You told me you saw a dog turn into a little canine Cage, of course it doesn't make sense. I'm just saying, maybe you're permanently mooned out."

"Oh. Damn," Stanley said. He hadn't considered that. Why would he have? But maybe that was the case. WereCage didn't mean werewolf. It made a sort of nonsense sense.

"But there's more!" Cameron said, excited that Stanley may have been on board with his point. He grabbed the aluminum bat and held it up.

"Your chain. You had it on when you got bit, and Cage sort of pushed it into your wound when he bit you, right?"

"Yeah, took a chunk out of me when I pulled it loose," Stanley agreed.

"So what if that's why you're different? You're still you, at least for part of the night, because the silver got in the wound. It kills werewolves! So maybe for you it diluted the whole Cage curse thing."

Stanley took the bat and held it up, looking at his chain wrapped around it alongside the older, slinkier ones.

"Oh man. Did you think of that yourself?" he asked.

"No," Cameron said. "I saw it in a movie when I was a kid. I think it really holds up to the passage of time in light of what's happening with you."

Despite Cam's answer, the idea made sense to Stanley. His necklace had been forced deeply into the bite at the moment it happened. It could have contaminated the bite, somehow caused the curse to not fully take hold. If not for that, he could have been a mindless Cage monster, just like the rest of them.

The St. Christopher's medal clinked as he turned the bat over in his hands. His father's chain had saved his life, maybe. Saved him from being just another in the horde of Cages that was on track to destroy the entire world. And now, as a weapon, maybe it would save everyone else. That was profound as hell.

Stanley smiled, feeling a real sense of confidence for the first time since everything had begun. He felt hope.

"This is going to work," he told Cameron.

"I sure hope so. I've never been to Montevideo, and it's been on my bucket list since forever."

Stanley put the bat down and went to his room, retrieving the length of paracord. He had Cameron help him look up the proper way to tie a lasso. Between the two of them, it took an hour to tie it properly so that it kept its shape and actually tightened when it was looped over someone and the end was pulled. Not a trap, but a useful tool for holding Bitey Cage still once he found him.

Cameron made lunch while Stanley researched therianthropy. There were more methods than he could have imagined for curing someone of lycanthropy and related conditions, but most of them sounded like the sorts of things that would just kill a person, anyway. In some stories, the person needed to be struck over the head with a knife. Others suggested dismemberment.

A common cure, or at least repellent, was wolfsbane, but Stanley had no idea where to even get something like that. Nails through palms and exorcisms were also cited. Calling the monster by its real name three times was even a possibility. There were more ways to cure lycanthropy than there were to cook a good steak. None of them were normal or easy to do.

They ate together and watched the movie *An American Werewolf in London*, which didn't do a lot to keep Stanley's confidence up. The ending left a lot to be desired, given his predicament.

"Look on the upside. The girl still loved him. Maybe Sara will be there when the police gun you down," Cameron told him as the end credits rolled.

"In this scenario, you're the rotting ghost friend that haunts me," Stanley pointed out. The werewolf in the film was haunted by his victims, including his best friend.

"Nah, I'm good. You have to kill me for me to haunt you."

"I don't think this kind of research is very helpful."

"Sure it is. You think the internet is any better? Or books? Hollywood has this market cornered and you turn into a Hollywood movie star. I think this is our only hope."

Cameron put on the movie *Dog Soldiers* next. It proved less helpful overall.

Stanley checked the time on his phone and cursed. It was already after five. He only had a couple of hours of sunlight left and then everything was going to start all over again.

"I have to start getting ready," he said. Cameron shook his head.

"One more movie," he insisted.

"Cam -"

"Stan, this could be it. You're going to drive yourself crazy. I know you. I know how you think. I can see the little wrinkles of stress in the corners of your eyes. I bet you already have to take a nervous shit, don't you? You need to sit here with me and relax and realize that things are going to happen. There's no preparation. There's just you and your instincts tonight. That's what you've got."

"Jesus, Cam, are you trying to make me throw up?"

"Stop. You're a good guy. You're not an action hero, or a genius, or a billionaire, and it doesn't matter. You'll do the right thing. I have faith in you."

It was arguably the nicest thing Cameron had ever told him, and he spoke the words without any of the vague sarcasm or teasing that so often tinged his speech. It was a genuine, real sentiment.

"Thank you, Cam."

"You're welcome. Now let's watch *Shaun of the Dead*."

He put the movie on despite it having nothing to do with werewolves and they watched and laughed together and Stanley managed to forget for a minute here and there that he was courting death that evening and likely would for every evening he remained alive from now on.

The sky was already growing darker as the movie came to an end. He felt the need to do something, the urge to prepare something, but in reality there was nothing to prepare. There was no plan other than to catch the other Cage. There was nothing to get ready besides the bat and the rope. The lack of plan made him as nervous as anything. He had done nothing all day long. And, worse, he knew there was nothing else he could have done.

"I should get my disguise, I guess," Stanley said then, looking out the window.

"Yeah. Pick something good. Grays and blacks. Nothing that stands out."

"I will," he agreed, heading to his room.

"Hey, Stanley?" Cameron called after him. He stopped at the doorway to his bedroom and looked back.

"Yeah?"

"I don't want to sound like a super gross sort of pervert, but when the time comes, can I watch?"

"What?"

"When you change. Can I watch?"

"Why would you want to do that?"

"Why would I want to watch my best friend magically turn into Nic Cage before he heads out to beat in the head of a different, eviler Nic Cage? I have no idea, Stan."

"Eviler isn't a word," Stanley told him.

"Stanley."

"Yeah," he said with a sigh. "You can watch."

"I'm getting some wine," Cameron said with no small degree of excitement.

In his room, Stanley found an old hoodie and a pair of sweatpants that he felt would make him look suitably unremarkable on any street. With a pair of sneakers and sunglasses, he'd look like a hundred other people. He'd be nobody, at least for as long as he could stop the Cage quotes from coming out.

With everyone hyper aware of the Nic Cage problem, he was hoping he'd be able to find Bitey Cage when he showed up. People had already made a "KillerCage" hashtag for what was happening, so he just set his phone to send him an alert when it started popping up again.

Stanley changed his clothes, hoping Nic Cage's body wouldn't find them ill-fitting and their ability to obscure his identity would remain intact. The light from his window grew dimmer by the moment. Night would fall soon enough. Nic Cage was coming.

He left his room once more. Cameron was set up on the sofa with a glass of wine, as promised. Stanley made sure the bat and the rope were ready, even though nothing could have happened to them in the interim.

"Almost time," Stanley said. Cameron looked at the windows.

"Yeah. If you don't want to do this, Stanley, I'll understand."

"It's fine. I don't care if you watch. It's probably pretty weird."

"Not that part. I absolutely want to watch that. I mean the rest. We're talking about it like you're planning a trip out of town for the weekend. But it's saving the world and maybe killing people. It's a lot to handle. Too much to handle."

He was surprised to hear it from Cameron. Not that Cameron was a "save the world" kind of guy. But the idea that he should just sit back and do nothing seemed wrong.

"How can I not at least try?"

"I'm just saying. We don't know what you're up against. What if there are already dozens? This may be a fight you can't win. No one can expect one man to stand up against the end of the world."

"Maybe they should," Stanley replied. He'd die for sure if he did nothing. So would Cameron. Sara. His mother. Gil at the market. He had to at least try.

"Maybe. But if you want a friend to watch the end of the world with, I'll be here."

Stanley was about to thank him when he felt the twist in his guts. The words he tried to speak died on his lips, replaced with a stunted groan as he doubled over.

"Stanley?" Cameron asked, sitting up.

He collapsed to his knees, the sour, burning taste filling his mouth. Cameron said something else, but the words were lost in the pain.

Bones snapped, and muscles stretched. He felt like he was being scrambled. Inside and out. He felt like he was dying and being remade, and maybe he was. If he really was immortal, maybe that would be his fate for the rest of eternity, to be torn apart every single night and remade in the image of a man he only knew as a pretend person, a character to fulfill a ninety-minute fantasy and nothing more. That was a hell of a curse he'd been afflicted with.

He screamed, trying to muffle the sound so as to not disturb the neighbors. Cameron tried to come to his aid, but he pushed him away, flailing blindly as his skull reshaped itself and his mind raced with thoughts that were barely his own.

The process felt like it took hours, like a lifetime of agony was heaped upon him and then, as suddenly as it had begun, it was gone once more. He lay panting on the floor, staring up at the popcorn ceiling of their apartment, Cameron's red and panicked face in his peripheral vision with eyes wide.

"Stanley, please say something if you're not dead," his roommate said.

"I dreamt I was as light as the ether. A floating spirit visiting things to come," he said quietly.

"Oh."

Stanley sat up and shook his head.

"No. That was Cage. I didn't mean that."

Stanley heard the words come out of his mouth in Nic Cage's voice. Felt Nic Cage's lips form them in Nic Cage's face. It was like wearing a mask that covered him utterly, inside and out. It made him feel like a stranger inside of his own head. And the most frightening part was that it still felt good. The power; the rush of it. It was exciting. Exciting and terrifying.

"Are you okay?"

"I'm fine," Stanley answered. "Once it's over, it's fine."

"It wasn't what I was expecting," Cameron told him.

"Me neither," Stanley said with a weak laugh.

He got to his feet then, stretching his arms and legs in the outfit he'd chosen for himself. He had torn the pants during his transformation, and the hoodie was too tight across the shoulders.

"I need to fix this," he said, returning to his room to find something else to wear. He didn't have a wide variety of things to choose from to fit the bill, but he did have his father's powder blue tuxedo that he bought for his wedding, which Stanley's mother refused to let him wear.

Stanley had never worn the tuxedo before and was never entirely sure why he'd kept it all these years, either. It was a piece of his dad and it was weird and he liked that. His dad, in a powder blue tux, was an image that made him smile and though he'd never seen the man in it, he wasn't sure his father had ever worn it at all. It was still something that connected them.

"What do you think?" he asked, leaving the room. The tux fit like a glove. Wide lapels framed a frilly shirt topped by a classy clip on bowtie. It was arguably the dressiest he had ever been in his life.

Cameron stared at him for a long moment.

"You were going to go out in disguise," he said finally. Stanley nodded.

"This is like a disguise. I've ever seen Nic Cage in a powder blue tuxedo."

"You sure you want to go in this direction? You're trying to not be shot tonight."

"I'll be fine," Stanley told him. He really liked the tux.

"Is that you talking, or Nic Cage?"

"It's me, obviously," he replied.

"And is that you or Nic Cage?"

Stanley grabbed the rope off of the kitchen island and the baseball bat.

"Please be careful, Stanley," Cameron told him.

He raised the bat to wave goodbye.

"I will. I'm going to finish this tonight. Somehow."

He headed out into the hallway, ready to get out into the night. Bitey Cage was out there somewhere. All of them were. And it was time to put an end to things.

## Chapter Twelve

The night was colder than the previous few had been when Stanley got to the street. The sky was partially cloudy and the diminishing moon was cutting in and out of view. The world smelled alive. Car exhaust, hot dogs, grass, people. The scents commingled in what could best be described as the smell of city.

Stanley slipped on a pair of sunglasses and headed down the street, baseball bat resting on his shoulder. Part of him knew he was doing the exact opposite of what he'd planned. This was not inconspicuous. This was fully conspicuous. But despite that realization, he still felt confident that it was a good idea.

A handful of pedestrians glanced in his direction and through his peripheral vision, he was able to catch one or two expressions of recognition. People knew who he was. His disguise was miserable at best. But fashionable. And oddly comfortable for a tuxedo. He felt good in it.

It was the influence of Cage, of that he was sure. Even in control of his own mind, as he was, the ideas were there. The Cage yearnings. The Caginess. It wanted out. It wanted to express itself. He had to try to keep that in check, but it was neither the time nor the place to worry about it. He had a world to save.

The first flash caught him off guard, and even with the sunglasses on, he blinked against the brightness. A man on the corner of the street had his phone up and rattled off a sequence of quick photos.

Someone shouted the name "Nic Cage" and soon other people were looking at him. Some ran, but most just retrieved their phones.

"You people should head home," Stanley said loudly, addressing those nearest him. "Things are gonna get weird."

*Was that a Nic Cage quote?* Stanley didn't think so. It sounded Cagey, though. Despite that, no one listened. More people snapped photos, and then the sound of a high-powered camera rattling off dozens of photos drew his attention.

A man in the crowd was using an expensive-looking camera with a massive lens, taking photo after photo. Stanley's eyes widened.

"Paparazzo!" he said accusingly. *Was that a Nic Cage quote?*

He was in danger of being shut down before he started. Somewhere in the distance, the wail of a siren had picked up. He'd already been ratted out, and he hadn't even reached the park yet. On the upside, causing a scene a few blocks from where he wanted to go would at least draw attention from where he needed to be. All he needed to do in the interim was to bridge the gap and get to the park unnoticed.

People shouted his name and someone threw half an iced coffee at him, spattering the drink across his pant legs. It would leave a stain, which he found disheartening. The mob of looky loos was slowly building confidence into just an old-fashioned mob.

Someone cursed at him, and another drink went flying. Angry faces yelled and someone suggested grabbing him. The man with the camera kept taking pictures.

Stanley didn't want to hurt anyone, but the crowd didn't share his benevolence. He needed to get away.

Flashing lights illuminated the street several blocks down as a police cruiser approached at full speed. He didn't have time to ponder a plan, he just needed to go.

He broke into a run. The crowd parted, fearful and unsure of what was happening as he barreled into the street. Cars honked, and a Mustang bore down on him, too close and too fast to brake in time.

Stanley jumped as the car approached, running across the hood to the roof and then jumping again. Nic Cage's jumping skills left Stanley's in the dust as he sailed from the Mustang to the roof of a Silverado and then leaped again onto the roof of a bus.

He ran the length of the bus and then jumped onto a parked SUV and finally the sidewalk on the opposite side of the road, a half block down from where he'd started. His feet kept moving, racing down the sidewalk and then cutting through an alleyway to the next street over.

The park was his ultimate destination, and he navigated the streets and alleys as quickly as he could, not giving people a chance to even see who he was or what he was doing. He hurdled parked vehicles and bounded off of moving ones like some kind of monkey weaving through trees in the jungle.

He approached the park at the location where he had been attacked originally, bounding down an alley between apartment buildings. The police presence was greater than he expected and the park was cordoned off, closed to the public. Officers were stationed at entrances, and at least a dozen cars were parked on that one street alone. He was certain the park was surrounded. They must have had every officer on the force working the area.

More photographers had taken up residence outside of the park as well, held back by police barricades. The crowd was greater than Stanley had anticipated. In truth, he hadn't anticipated a crowd at all.

Standing around and thinking of what to do had done nothing for him so far, so he chose to not do it anymore. He let his momentum keep him going. It would work.

"I'm super powered Nic Cage," he said as he sprang from the shadows concealing himself and a dumpster in the alley. "I'm immortal!"

He raced across the street, drawing all eyes towards himself. Photographers shouted and raced to get a better position. The four police officers at the main entrance drew weapons and yelled at him to get to his knees. Cars honked and swerved aside.

"I'm saving the world!" Stanley shouted back. He jumped from the street to the hood of a police cruiser and then from the cruiser across the sidewalk and over a small fence into the park itself.

The police gave chase, radioing Stanley's position to backup. He didn't wait to see how many were following or from where. He just ran, the wind in his receding hair and a manic smile on his face.

"I'm saving the world!" he yelled at the top of his lungs. It was not Cage yelling. It was Stanley Miller. And it felt amazing.

He stormed through trees and down a path, quickly outpacing the police. Lights flashed near and far through the park, signs that he was not able to slow down or think himself safe. There were dozens of them, more police than he had ever seen in one place at one time. They'd shoot him, he knew that, just like they'd shot Raging Cage and Bitey Cage. But he was going to make them work for it.

A gunshot rang out somewhere ahead of him and Stanley stumbled, fearful he'd been hit. There was no pain, however. Another shot and another filled the darkness. And another sounded from further away. They were not firing at him. The other Cages had to be in the park. Some of them, at least.

Stanley sprinted towards the pond. He couldn't let the police take out Bitey Cage. He didn't think they'd be able to kill him. There was no mention that Raging Cage had died the night before, despite being shot. But they could wound him and capture him and make it a lot harder for Stanley to get his work done. He needed to find him first.

He got off the path and chose to run through the woods to provide a little more cover, at least until he reached the pond. With all the bullets flying around, taking some extra caution couldn't hurt. Even if bullets wouldn't kill him, he bet they still felt bad.

Leaves and twigs crunched under his heavy footfalls. More shots filled the night, one much closer than the others. Stanley took a sharp turn, angling towards the sound in case there was a Cage nearby and ran headlong into another man in the woods.

The two of them fell down, Stanley holding his head where his skull had knocked against the other man's.

"What the hell?" he muttered, pulling fingers tinged with blood away.

"It's okay, Eleanor. It can be fixed," the other man said.

"I'm a baaaaaad man," a third, higher-pitched voice added. Stanley grimaced and watched as Raging Cage and Dog Cage got to their feet. Raging Cage was bleeding from his stomach, but Dog Cage seemed fine, though he still had a leash and collar around his neck.

"Where's the other guy? The other Cage?" Stanley asked.

"I am not here to force my twisted soul into your life," Raging Cage said, his voice a strained whisper. He held his own stomach as blood poured through his fingers. Maybe they weren't immortal at all.

A thundering sound that steadily grew louder preceded a bright light that slashed through the night from above. A police helicopter had joined the search as dozens of flashlights on the ground closed in on their position.

Stanley cursed, looking for a way out that wouldn't get him shot. Above them, a second helicopter joined the first and someone shouted over the sound of the whirring blades. A light hit Stanley in the face. Even with the sunglasses, it obscured his ability to see who was wielding it. Not that it mattered, of course. He knew they'd been found.

"I think when I'm done with this I'll have a gin and tonic," Raging Cage said. He laughed then and turned around, facing the approaching police. With a scream he began to run. Stanley ducked down, grabbing Dog Cage's leash to prevent the tiny man from joining the slaughter, as gunshots rang out from multiple angles.

Raging Cage's body twitched and danced like a puppet on strings. Bullets ripped his flesh apart. In the light cast by the helicopters, Stanley could see sprays of blood exploding left and right, high and low. His body was spun completely around and for a brief moment, the two Cages made eye contact. Raging Cage grinned and the front of his face burst open as a bullet tore through from the back of his head. Blood, skull and brains splattered across Stanley's face as the other man's body fell to the ground.

"Oh, Christ! Oh Christ, where am I?" Dog Cage pleaded, pulling at the leash. Stanley reined him in, hugging the squirming little man against his tux as the cops rushed towards them. He may have looked like a small, naked Nicolas Cage, but he was just a dog trying to go to his master. Stanley didn't want him to die.

The two of them were surrounded quickly. Guns and lights filled the darkness, all directed at Stanley. He raised his hands while Dog Cage whimpered.

"Oh Jesus, what the hell is that?" one of the police officers asked.

"Shut up and cuff them," someone else said. A third voice began reading Stanley his rights while others shouted orders. Someone hit him on the side of the head with the butt of a gun and knocked him down. His face was pushed into the dirt and leaves as handcuffs were fixed to his wrists. Dog Cage struggled, shouting movie quotes until the zap of a taser going off shut him down completely. They handcuffed his tiny wrists and dragged them both to their feet.

As they were pulled from the park, Stanley could see that the second helicopter was not police, but news. More camera vans lined the streets and lights flooded the park entrance, filming him and Dog Cage as they were taken to a police cruiser and tossed in the back.

Dog Cage had yet to come to, and his limp body was tossed on the seat next to Stanley. Police pushed through the crowds of onlookers and reporters. An officer got into the driver's seat and another in the passenger seat. They drove off quickly, sirens blaring and lights flashing.

"Why the hell is there a little one?" the officer in the passenger seat asked his partner. Stanley made eye contact with him in the rearview mirror.

"I ain't asking questions," the driver stated.

"But it's him. How the hell is there a little one?"

"Raines, man, I ain't asking questions," the driver said more emphatically. Raines turned around in his seat. He looked pale and sweaty. He stared at Stanley.

"What the hell is that thing?" he asked, nodding to Dog Cage. Stanley said nothing.

"Just leave him," the driver said. "We got him, s'all that matters."

"All that matters?" Raines said, turning back in his seat. "We blew that guy to pieces and they say he's still got a pulse. A pulse and the same goddamn face as these two! What the hell is going on?"

The driver glanced at Raines, his expression stern and surly. He said nothing, and Raines shook his head, looking back at the road.

Stanley had never been to the police station before. Had he given it any thought in the past, he certainly wouldn't have guessed that his first visit would be under these circumstances.

The officers drove the car around back and into an underground garage, away from any potential cameras and gawkers. They pulled up alongside a reinforced door and pulled Stanley out roughly. Dog Cage was awake but docile now. He growled and muttered quiet Nic Cage quotes but said little else. They had taken his leash and collar and now he was simply a very small, naked man. It was unsettling in the extreme.

Stanley and Dog Cage were taken down a concrete hallway into a room full of a dozen holding cells. There were a handful of other men present, some passed out and others sitting or standing around. All eyes were on Stanley and Dog Cage when they entered.

"In," the driver of the car said, opening an empty cell and pushing Stanley inside. Dog Cage growled and Raines pushed him to the ground at Stanley's feet before the cell door was locked behind them.

"Those officers you killed the other day were good men," the driver said to Stanley. He must have meant the ones that Raging Cage and Dog Cage had taken out after Stanley's selfie with them. He was surprised to hear they were dead and hadn't turned. Unless they had and these men just didn't know it yet.

Stanley wanted to tell them it wasn't him, that he had been trying to fix everything, but he didn't. Instead, he said nothing. Trying to explain things here and now would just make it worse.

"Don't you want your phone call, Cage?" Raines asked. "Get your Hollywood lawyer in here?"

Dog Cage growled and sat on the floor, his legs spread obscenely.

"You're never seeing the light of day again. We got you dead to rights. Dead to rights, man," Raines told him, the anger clear as day in his voice.

"Come on," the driver told the other officer. They left together, the heavy door locking behind them. Stanley sighed loudly and looked across the remaining holding cells. The other prisoners looked as shocked and confused as Raines had. Some of those that shared cells talked quietly to one another.

Stanley turned and took a seat on the small bench that was attached to the wall. Dog Cage watched him go and then proceeded to circle the cell, smelling the bars and the corners. When he got to the toilet, he took a drink from the bowl, his little hands holding him steady on the rim, causing some of the other prisoners to groan.

There were no windows in the holding cell and no clock, either. It had been early when Stanley went out, but he knew, trapped in the cell, the minutes would tick by fast enough. When morning came, he was going to have a seriously hard time explaining himself to the police.

He sat on the bench and stared at the floor. Some of the other prisoners worked up the nerve to yell at him a few times, but he didn't respond. He wanted no part of anything else, not that night. His plan, such as it was, had been a splendid failure. A police helicopter was an unexpected twist. He didn't even know they had a helicopter.

Raines indicated Raging Cage was still alive, despite what should have killed him several times over. Stanley's face was still splattered with the contents of the man's head. They had given him nothing with which to clean up. If he was still alive, then it was likely the two dead police officers were not as dead as everyone thought. Maybe they were out rampaging through the night right at that moment alongside Bitey Cage. Maybe some of the other injured from the night before were out as well. The numbers were growing, just like Wilford Brimley predicted.

There was no way to tell how much time had passed, but Stanley was sure it was hours before he finally heard something beyond the holding cell block doors. There was a loud bang from somewhere within the police precinct. The other prisoners perked up, and Dog Cage, who had curled up near Stanley's feet, stood up as well.

"You heard that too, huh?" Stanley asked. Dog Cage produced a low growl and mumbled something from *Ghost Rider*.

A series of pops went off, muffled by the stone walls. Stanley was certain they were gunshots. Another bang and something shook the entire building. The other men shared nervous glances, and a series of additional gunshots sounded closer. Screaming then, close but muffled, and something thudded against the door.

The small window set into the door flashed red suddenly. Blood ran down the outside and something hit it hard. The door shook and dust fell from the ceiling above it. Another bang, and then another, and the door collapsed inward, landing with a heavy thud on the concrete floor.

Dust billowed and more gunshots sounded deeper in the building. People screamed and a police officer's body was thrown into the room. It slammed against the bars of a holding cell and crumpled in a motionless, bloody heap.

As the dust of the door settled, the silhouette of a figure appeared. A man, walking purposefully. He entered the room and stepped into the light. Nic Cage's smiling face scanned the room and settled on Stanley.

Three more figures burst into the room behind him, running quickly and darting from cell to cell. Each one bore Nic Cage's face, though they were all dressed differently and one, in a police uniform, had a bullet wound in his shoulder.

The three Cages were almost manic, scrambling from cell to cell, smelling the bars and grimacing at the prisoners held within. They muttered Cage quotes or laughed for no discernible reason as the first Cage, the quiet and calm one, walked across the room to Stanley's cell.

Dog Cage ran to the cell door, holding the bars as best he could in his small hands, looking up at the new Cage. He whimpered and the new Cage reached two fingers down to scrub the top of his head. Dog Cage grinned and leaned into the attention.

"How's your evening going?" Cage asked Stanley. It was not Bitey Cage, but there was still something oddly familiar about this one, beyond the obvious.

"Been better," Stanley admitted. Cage's smile widened, and his eyes darted away from Stanley to the bars of the cell.

"Little bit of a pickle, huh?"

"A whole jar of them."

Cage laughed.

"That's good. I like that. I do like you, you know?"

He said the words as though he expected that Stanley was afraid the opposite was true. It was weird, but so was everything that was happening. Stanley approached the cell door, looking the new Cage up and down. He wore a t-shirt and what looked like they might have been yoga pants.

"Do I know you?" Stanley asked. Cage chuckled, and the other Cages howled with laughter, stumbling over random and irrelevant quotes from movies. Even Dog Cage giggled.

"I'm Nic Cage, can't you tell?"

Stanley's eyes narrowed. New Cage wasn't wearing any shoes. He looked like all the rest otherwise, however, save for a pair of earrings. Still, even his manner of speech seemed to be like he was telling a joke that Stanley wasn't getting.

"You're like me," Stanley said. "Not the others. You're you in there, whoever you are." The new Cage didn't speak in quotes. He was clear headed and in control. Stanley didn't think he'd meet another one like him.

"Obviously," Cage agreed. "I imagine I have you to thank for that."

Stanley didn't understand what the man meant at first. But there was only one real possibility.

"You're the one that bit me," he said. Cage's smile widened.

"Look at you, figuring stuff out without even Googling it," he said. It still didn't make sense, though. If he was level-headed, why bite Stanley in the first place?

He scanned the man's face as if he'd see some secret message written there. The wide eyes, the familiar hairline, the tiny earrings shaped like moons. The same pair he'd seen once before.

"Sara?" Stanley whispered. Cage laughed, his eyes as wide and manic as they could ever get. His hands gripped the bars of the cell.

"I know, right? It's crazy!"

Stanley could only stare in dumb silence for a long, drawn out moment. Sara's earrings. Sara herself, behind Nic Cage's eyes. She was the one that bit him. Bitey Cage was just another random, like Raging Cage. She was the real one.

"I don't understand."

"I don't blame you. It's a bit of a mind bender. But that chain of yours saved my life. Yours too, right? When I bit you, when that silver punctured my gums and the roof of my mouth, everything sort of snapped into place. I was me again. I was Nic Cage, but I was me. It's a little blurry, but you probably get what I mean."

"You bit me," he stated. She nodded.

"Yeah, definitely. Not me, really. Nic Cage. But it was a good thing I did. You're the only other one who gets it. The only other one that can see the world through your own eyes and Nic Cage's."

"Well, what the hell? What are you doing?" he asked, pointing to the crumpled body of the cop on the floor. Sara shrugged.

"What do you mean?"

"You killed that cop! People keep getting attacked. Why aren't you stopping it?"

Sara rolled her eyes as though the question were the dumbest thing ever.

"Stanley, why would I stop? You're feeling what I'm feeling, too. I know you are. This is amazing. Life as Nic Cage? It's a goddamn rush."

"You killed that guy!" he pointed to the cop again. Sara shrugged.

"Eggs and omelets, Stanley. I figured you'd get this. You're literally the only person in the world who can."

"Don't you want to stop it? End the curse?" he asked her. She laughed again and the assorted Cages laughed with her.

"You have to be kidding. I have never felt anything like this in my life. The power of being in this body. And look, all of these others, they do what I want them to do. I control them. I'm the master here. I can run everything!"

"The Alpha Cage," Stanley muttered. She snapped her fingers and pointed at him.

"Damn right, Stanley. The Alpha Cage. Do you know how many times I've been the Alpha anything in my life? I don't want to sound too full of myself here, but this is a real opportunity for me to fix the dumbassery that everyone else in the world has done."

"What the hell does that even mean? You're killing people."

"Oh my God, Stanley, calm down. I don't kill people. Do any of these people look dead?"

"That guy!" Stanley said, pointing at the cop again. With a frown, Sara gestured and one of the other Cages approached the cop's body. He rolled it over, showing off a bite on the officer's hand.

"See? Not dead. He'll come back tomorrow or the next day right as rain. I'm not a killer. I'm a fixer. I'm making everyone better."

"How is this better?"

"It's Nic Cage! You love Nic Cage. You were at that film festival just like me. How is it not better? Aren't you faster now? Stronger?"

"I don't want to be a faster, stronger Nic Cage. If you keep doing this, do you have any idea how fast it'll spread?"

She scoffed and rolled her eyes at him.

"I understand math, Stanley," she assured him. "And so what? Imagine what I could get done if every night everyone turned into a super powered Nic Cage that I could control?"

"I don't even know what that means. What are you getting done?" he asked.

"I don't know. Critical infrastructure. Low income housing. Wind farms and solar panels. An end to crime. It's an army of powerful Nic Cages, Stanley. Try to think outside the box. Whatever people during the day keep screwing up, I can make better at night."

"Jesus, you want to wield an army of superpowered, altruistic WereCages?"

"Still using that word, huh?" she said.

He wanted to call her a monster, but wasn't even sure it fit. She wanted to make the world a better place. It was just so obviously the wrong way to do it. How could she not see that?

Stanley looked down at his own blood-splattered, powder blue suit. Of course she couldn't see that she was planning something ridiculous and wrong. In her head, it probably sounded totally reasonable. The Cage influence was tricky. If it wasn't blue tuxedos, it was world domination through charitable deeds.

"But it's hurting people. Even if they survive. You're taking their autonomy away. Their self!"

"Eh, they'll be fine," she countered. Not the strongest argument Stanley had ever heard, but she seemed convinced. "During the day, everyone gets to be themselves. It's just at night I get to be King Cage and fix everything. I can't really see a downside."

"I just... how did you know I'd be at the clinic? Is this why you asked me to dinner?"

"The clinic? No, that was just a weird coincidence. And dinner was just that. I thought we could have a nice time. Didn't know we'd be going all Cage every night regardless of the moon status, though. I didn't even make it to the restaurant, but I gather from your message you didn't either."

"No," he replied. He was oddly relieved that he hadn't actually stood her up. But, given what he now knew, it wasn't as much of a relief as it could have been.

"You're holding yourself back in life, Stanley. Take the bull by the horns. We could do a lot of good together."

"What you're doing isn't right," he stated. She snorted and grabbed the cell door, yanking it from the hinges as though it were made of cheap plastic. She tossed it aside.

"Could have left any time you wanted. All you had to do was try," she told him. "You need to stop standing in your own way."

"Who says I'm in my own way?" he asked.

"Oh, Stanley," she said with a shake of her head. She stepped towards him until they were nose to nose. Nic Cage's eyes stared into his. She turned her head ever so slightly and leaned in, giving him a kiss. One of the other prisoners grunted.

"I think you're a good guy, Stanley," she said, pulling away from him. "But you need to decide who you want to be in life."

She turned away from him then, and the other Cages ran from the room while she followed behind. In the doorway, she stopped once more, looking back at him.

"Dawn's coming, Stanley. Dawn and more police."

She ran then, after the others, and into the depths of the police station. Stanley looked down at Dog Cage. The tiny version of Nic Cage smiled up at him expectantly. He gave him a pat on the head and looked at the other prisoners in the room.

"Dude," the nearest man said. Stanley didn't want to hear it. He leaned over and picked up Dog Cage, cradling the little man in his left arm as he ran from the holding cell.

The police station looked like a war zone. There was smoke in the halls from a fire that Stanley couldn't see, but that seemed to be the least of the problems. Whole walls had been knocked down, doors torn from their hinges. The halls and rooms were littered with bodies, though Stanley saw clear bite marks on every one he inspected. They would all return. The Brimley numbers would be way off if Sara was turning this many people every night.

He fled through the garage, out onto the street. The city was pandemonium. Sirens blared near and wide, and fires burned in the night. It was as though the world had come to an end while he was held in the cell.

Cars were piled up out front of the police station, a multi-vehicle accident with every participant looking like a corpse either in their vehicle or on the road nearby. Bite marks on everyone. Sara and her crew had been thorough and terrible in their sweeping of the place. By the next night there would be hundreds of Cages, not just a handful.

The sky was already showing signs of growing lighter in the east as Stanley made his way through the chaos, trying to keep out of sight as best he could. The adrenaline was finally beginning to slip away, and he found Nic Cage becoming harder to resist at the back of his mind. He wondered if it had been the fear and uncertainty of the night that had kept him at bay for so long. The other nights, he had lost himself much sooner. Now it seemed like he had a chance to make it all the way to dawn with his own mind.

He ran down alleys whenever he could and side streets as much as possible. The police station was far from his apartment and he wasn't fully clear on the way to go. Police cars and fire trucks still zipped through the city in pursuit of other Cages, perhaps, or the fires that someone was setting. Stanley avoided them all, creeping through the shadows.

He was in sight of his own neighborhood when the first light of dawn started to appear on the horizon. The pain of the transformation returned and Stanley collapsed in an alley alongside a trio of restaurant trash cans.

Dog Cage howled and writhed, and Stanley did the same, gritting his teeth. He was suddenly very glad he had never been conscious for the change back before and the thought grew hazy in his own head. He had been hasty in that opinion; it seemed. His vision went black, and the pain faded to a dull numbness and then, finally, nothing at all.

## Chapter Thirteen

Stanley woke with water splashing on his face. He grunted and wiped it away, and another drop hit. He stared up at the end of some kind of exhaust pipe venting condensation from the side of a brick building. The next drop hit him square in the forehead.

He sat up, wiping his face again, and looked around. The sky was blue, though he was in a darkened alley. His tuxedo was stained with dirt and alley goo and the dried brains of Raging Cage. He felt like crap.

A small, curly-haired black dog leapt into his lap and stood on its hind legs, looking him in the face. It must have weighed about ten pounds, and its face was mostly obscured in a thicket of black curls.

"Dog Cage?" he said. The animal wagged its tail and made a quiet grunting sound. He took the dog in his arms and stood up. He had to get home.

In the light of day, the city was no better than it had seemed at night. Smoke filled the air and police cars raced up and down streets. There were more helicopters in the air and the sense of unease from the few people on the streets was palpable.

Stanley made it home quickly, drawing less attention than a man in a filthy blue tux cradling a dog should have. People had more things on their mind and, since he didn't look like Nic Cage any longer, they had no time to waste on him.

He raced up to the apartment and let himself in, still holding the dog. Cameron was on the couch at his computer, the curtains drawn.

"Oh my God, Stanley," he said, standing and looking aghast.

"Yeah," he agreed, though he wasn't sure what he was agreeing to.

"Your face. Is that blood? Is that your blood?"

"No. Nic Cage," he answered. Cameron looked at the dog. "This is Dog Cage."

"It's an actual dog."

"It's an actual dog," he agreed. He had yet to move from the doorway and then, finally, he bent over and let the dog go. Dog Cage wagged his tail and made a frantic bid for the kitchen, sniffing everything he could find.

"You and that ridiculous tuxedo were all over the internet," Cameron told him. "You're on the news in Kenya, for God's sake. They made memes about the dog. It's the craziest thing I have ever seen."

"What the hell happened? The fires and the helicopters and everything," Stanley asked.

"There were dozens of them out there. Nic Cages. The FBI is here, there's talk of calling in the National Guard. Actual Nic Cage went missing from Bulgaria. There's a

State of Emergency. It's like the end of the goddamn world. Only it *is* the end of the goddamn world, but no one knows about it."

"It's worse," Stanley told him, heading to the sink and turning on the tap. He splashed water in his face and tried to rinse the dried insides of Raging Cage's head from his face.

"You can't say that and then not finish your thought," Cameron said from the far side of the kitchen island. Dog Cage ran across the room, smelling the rest of the furniture.

"I found Alpha Cage, and it's Sara," Stanley said into the sink.

"Nurse Sara?" Cameron gasped. Stanley looked back over his shoulder.

"Yeah. She busted me out of jail."

Cameron sat on one of the stools.

"I need more than this."

Stanley turned around, wiping himself off on a paper towel.

"It was my chain. The silver didn't just keep me clear-headed, it did the same to her. So she bit me and then got her senses, only she's a friggin' loon."

"I don't think we're using that word," Cameron told him.

"She's doing this on purpose. She's the Alpha, so all the others do her bidding. She can control them. She wants to turn everyone into Nic Cage so she can rule the world at night."

"Oh, then no. That's loon stuff for sure. We probably don't need a murderous She-Cage running the world in darkness."

"Right?" Stanley agreed, getting a glass of water. "I mean, in fairness, she hasn't actually murdered anyone. And she wants to do things like install solar power and make the Nic Cages build affordable housing."

He took a sip of water and looked at Cameron, who simply stared back at him.

"One more time?" he said.

"She sorta wants to use them to do good deeds. On a global scale. At night."

"Huh," Cameron said. "That's something. Less villainous than I imagined at first."

"Yeah, no. I agree with you. I feel like it's still evil, but I don't know why."

"Heard," Cameron agreed with a nod. "I mean, the control part is wrong."

"Lack of autonomy, I told her that."

"Didn't phase her?" Cameron asked. Stanley drank more and shook his head.

"No, not really. I think it's Cage. Like, when you turn, he sneaks into your mind a little. Makes you act a little odd."

"Oh good, you noticed that," his roommate said, pointing to his dirty blue tuxedo.

"Yeah. I think she's still a good person in there. I mean, she has to be, right?"

"Global domination towards the end of affordable housing seems kind of good, maybe," Cameron agreed.

"Lower crime rates, too. Infrastructure, that sort of thing."

"Like a real full scale social program to benefit everyone?"

"Think so," Stanley said.

"Huh."

There was silence between them again. Outside, sirens continued to wail near and far.

"Like, right now, it seems like this is not happening. With the fires and the murders," Cameron pointed out.

"But they're not technically murders. They come back."

"Granted. I'm just saying, from an optics point of view. She could have maybe gone about it differently."

"It's hard not to be impulsive as Nic Cage."

"I can only imagine," Cameron told him.

"Yeah. I need to stop her. I just don't know how. I lost the bat and the rope last night. And Raging Cage's face exploded onto mine and he's still alive, so we really are immortal."

"Oh!" Cameron exclaimed, getting up quickly. Dog Cage barked as he ran to his own room. Stanley finished his glass of water while Cameron thumped around in his room. After a moment, he returned brandishing a pie server.

"Pie?" Stanley said.

"Sterling silver. From my grandma's set."

"Oh, cool. I can, I don't know. Bonk her in the head."

"Or," Cameron suggested, "we can sharpen it and you can stab her."

"Even better." He stifled a yawn and watched as Dog Cage circled the kitchen island before opening the fridge and pulling a leftover pork chop out, tossing it on the floor for the dog.

"Oh, fun, we're throwing meat on the floor now. Just embracing the chaos," Cameron said.

"Sorry," Stanley said. Cameron waved his hands dismissively.

"Don't worry. You go get cleaned. Burn that tuxedo and then maybe sleep. I'll sharpen up your weapon here and feed this dog that we're absolutely not keeping."

"I can't sleep. I have to find Sara."

"Where? Do you know her address?"

"I can Google it," Stanley replied. He felt like it wasn't a creeper move to do that now. It was in the interests of saving the world.

"Her address is not going to be online. This isn't nineteen ninety-five. Just get cleaned and sleep and I'll get you up before the circus starts again."

"Cam -"

"Stanley, seriously. I'm not trying to be like heroic or motherly. You smell like absolute garbage and I want you to just go somewhere and not smell. Please. Sorry."

"Oh," Stanley said. That made sense. Brains and alley trash were not the best combo. He headed into his room while Dog Cage gnawed on the pork chop. He was sad to see that his dad's tuxedo had been pretty much ruined, but at least he got to wear it once.

He tossed the tux into his bathroom garbage after getting undressed and got into the shower. He felt like he could sleep for a week, but he knew that time was not on his side. He knew that Sara was out there and she knew he'd be looking for her. The night would be full of Cages. At the rate they were going, the city would be overrun in a matter of days. All that stood between humanity and a future of weirdly helpful subjugation was a sharp pie server and Stanley's wits. The odds were looking grim.

He had to wash his hair twice to get all the brains out, and when he was finished, he simply flopped into his bed. Sleep was fast to overtake him.

No sooner had Stanley closed his eyes than a flurry of wet and sloppy movements brought him back to his senses. The light in the room had changed considerably and Dog Cage stood on his chest, licking his face from chin to nose.

He grunted, rolling over and forcing the dog to hop off and sit on the bed next to him. His eyes adjusted to the clock at his bedside. It was nearly five o'clock in the evening. He had slept the entire day away.

"You need something?" he muttered. Dog Cage grunted and pawed at him. He doubted Cameron had taken him out. The little guy probably needed to pee something fierce.

Stanley dressed quickly and left his room with the dog at his heels. Cameron was still on the couch with his computer.

"You're up," he said.

"Yeah. This guy needs to go, I think."

"Is that what he was doing? I'm not good with dogs, but he was definitely scratching at the door."

Stanley sighed and nodded. He looked around the kitchen and finally settled on an extension cord from the hall closet that he looped over the dog's head as a makeshift leash.

"We'll be back in a few minutes, I guess."

"The streets seem pretty crazy still. Try not to get shot," his roommate advised.

"Will do," Stanley agreed, heading out. He led Dog Cage down the stairs and out the front door onto the street. The dog peed on the corner of the doorway right away, standing with a leg lifted. Stanley watched cars go by and breathed in the still lingering smell of smoke. There were no police in his neighborhood, but he had no doubt that everything from the night before had hit the fan on a much bigger level. If the FBI was already in town, things were only going to keep escalating. He wondered if the military would respond to a plague of Nic Cages. They'd fail, of course, but they'd still try.

He felt bad for real Nic Cage. Cameron had said he'd gone missing. Stanley didn't blame him. If his face was being spread like a virus, he might go into hiding, too. It was ruining the man's good name. Stanley wasn't sure he qualified as the biggest victim in all of this, but he was certainly one of them.

Dog Cage finished peeing and joined Stanley at his side. He started down the sidewalk at a leisurely pace. The dog seemed very accepting of his makeshift leash, so Stanley decided to take him around the block.

They reached the end of the street, and Stanley took the left turn. He stopped short, nearly running right over someone standing in his way.

"You're making it too easy, Stanley," Sara said. Before he could say anything, he heard the snap of the taser and felt the jolt run through his body, causing him to seize up and collapse.

She knelt down over him and pulled a syringe out from a small bag, flicking it once and then sticking him in the neck with it. He kept trying to speak, but no words would come out.

"Don't worry, I'm a nurse, remember? You'll be fine."

Her smile was the last thing he saw as his vision went black.

*\*\**

*I'm a match, she's kerosene*
*You know she's gonna burn down everything*

Stanley blinked his eyes as the song continued playing somewhere behind him. He was in a room he didn't recognize. The walls were white, and the carpet was a silvery gray. There was a massive painting of what looked like Tom Waits fighting a snake on the wall above a sofa. Dog Cage was curled up underneath it.

"Where am I?" he asked, trying to move. His arms and legs wouldn't respond. He was seated and tied in place.

"Oh, hey," Sara's voice replied. She came into the room with a yogurt and a spoon in her hands. "You're up. That was fast. Good metabolism."

"What's going on?" he asked her. She ate a spoonful of yogurt.

"This is my place. Figured I'd bring you here to keep you out of trouble for a while."

"I can't believe you're like this during the day, too," he said. He was hoping it was just Cage messing with her head. There was no excuse during the light of day. None except her being a nutter.

"This is a complicated thing, Stanley. I never meant to bite you. I never wanted that. I didn't even know I did it until after I did it. I couldn't remember what I did as Cage until after the silver in that bite cleared my head. But I get it now. It's a real opportunity for me. I just can't have another clearheaded Cage in the mix. You get that, right?"

"So you're going to kill me?" he asked. She ate some more yogurt and frowned at him.

"What is that, the fifth time you've accused me of murder? Are you dead? Do you feel dead? I'm not killing you. I tied you to a chair in my living room. I put on the Interrupters for you and it's a killer album, but it's not a murderer's album."

He shook his head, confused and tired and not just from whatever she'd injected him with.

"I just don't understand why you think enslaving literally all of mankind is not a bad thing."

"It's not enslavement. Geez, loaded word, too. It's creative positioning through unique opportunity."

"Sara, come on. This can't be who you are."

"Says who? You? You barely know me, Stan. I'm a girl you met at her job for like fifteen minutes once. Twice. I'm sorry if you built me up to be someone else in your head, but the fact is I'm doing this for me. For the real me. This is me being important for the first time ever. This is me being powerful for the first time ever."

"I understand that, trust me -"

"Hold your 'me too' horses. You don't understand. You understand what it means to be Nic Cage powerful. I could have done the MCATs, could have been a doctor, but I wanted to be a nurse. Thought I could help more people, really get to know them and be there for them. Instead, I get doctors talking down to me, senior nurses treating me like I'm an idiot, patients acting like I'm a waitress. Even you, stumbling all over yourself because 'oh my God, pretty girl.' It's been that way my whole life. No one takes me seriously. No one listens. Well, guess what? They're not going to have the choice much longer."

She finished her yogurt angrily and Stanley sighed.

"I'm sorry people treat you like that. Or if you thought I treated you like that."

"It's the way people are, Stanley. And it sucks. But look, I found a way to get past it. I found a way to make things better. So why are you pissing on my parade?"

"Pissing on your parade? I'm just trying to save the world."

Sara laughed at him and it wasn't the sort of evil laugh one expects from a world-destroying monster. It just sounded like she legitimately thought what he said was funny. It was annoyingly cute, and he was not amused that he thought so.

"It's adorable and very sweet that you think that. But listen, I'm trying to save the world, too. Your way leaves everything exactly the way it's been. Poverty and homelessness and violence and misery. My way fixes all of that. I don't want to say I have a better idea than you, but, you know... I really do. And I think we've just run out of time on the day."

She crossed the room to a window and drew aside the curtains. The sky was dark, with the faintest hints of light just barely visible in the distance as the sun set over the horizon. She grabbed a baseball bat from next to the window and lifted it up. Stanley recognized his father's St. Christopher medal and the other silver chains he and Cameron had wrapped around it.

"This is pretty cool, I have to say," she said, showing him the bat. "Snagged it from the cops last night. I really do like you, Stanley. But there's no room for two Alpha Cages in this town."

She lifted the bat, testing her grip. Stanley struggled against his bonds. He rocked and shook his body, but the ropes were tight and well-tied.

"You don't have to do this," Stanley told her. "You're a nurse, for God's sake. If you do this, you'll for real be murdering someone."

"I'm not killing anyone," she told him. "Nic Cage is."

She turned to watch the sky again as the last vestiges of the sun faded away. She stumbled back just as Stanley felt the twisting in his own guts. Dog Cage howled, rolling over on the sofa and writhing belly up. The three of them began their transformation as one. Bones shifted and joints popped audibly. The pain was clearly as acute for them as it was for Stanley.

Sara's body expanded like a balloon made of flesh. Her shoulders, arms, torso and thighs all pushed out, bulging and writhing like faceless meat monsters struggling to be born. Her skull popped with a sound like a fallen melon and her eyes spread apart, the orbital bones expanding to allow the eyes themselves to grow bigger.

Stanley watched the teeth shift in her mouth, the lips thin and spread wider across her face. Even her skin tone changed while the bones and muscles rearranged themselves into someone new.

Despite the transition, the ropes with which Stanley had been bound were too well tied. Even as his mass shifted and reformed, the ropes moved and rolled with him. He remained secured even after it was all over.

Sara stood when it was done, no longer the woman he had been so enamored with at the clinic but Nic Cage. Dog Cage sat on the sofa, his little feet dangling over the edge. All three were the same now.

"Now where were we?" Sara said in Cage's voice. She took a step towards Stanley with the bat and then stopped as someone knocked on the door.

"Help!" Stanley yelled.

"Just kidding," Sara yelled in the same voice. "Come back later."

"No, not later. She's trying to kill me!"

"Is what I'd say if there was a woman in here," Sara finished for him.

The knock came again, and Sara frowned.

"Can you just -" she began. The door burst in, the lock breaking through the wood of the frame as a man forced his way into the room. Stanley was not surprised to see it was Nic Cage in a leather jacket and in desperate need of a shave.

"Excuse me," Sara said, looking at her broken door. "What the hell is this?"

"What the hell is this?" new Cage replied, taking in the visual of Nic Cage tied to a chair while Nic Cage held a baseball bat like a weapon and a small Nic Cage watched from the sofa.

"I don't need any of you right now. Go play or something," Sara told him. New Cage smiled and pointed at Dog Cage.

"Weirdest thing in the room, right?" he said.

"Out," Sara insisted. She approached him with her hand out to push him out the door and he stopped her, taking her wrist in his hand.

"What the hell?" she asked.

"This the hell," Cage replied. With his other hand, he stuck her in the neck with a syringe full of a viscous looking gray liquid. Her jaw dropped and her eyes widened as she tried to reach for either the syringe or her own neck. Her hand flopped down uselessly before she reached either, and her body collapsed as though she'd been knocked out.

Sara began to spasm, slowly at first and then violently. A series of groans and strained cries escaped her lips, and then the change began to overtake her once more. The process reversed itself, her hair growing longer and blonde again even as her skull shrank and muscles receded beneath her flesh. In moments, Sara was passed out on the floor.

Pain overwhelmed Stanley, and the process began again for him as well. Dog Cage flopped to the floor, returning to his canine form while Stanley reverted to himself. When it was over, the new Nic Cage was still standing in the center of the room.

"That was wild," Cage said, approaching Stanley. He began to untie the ropes holding him to the chair.

"What just happened? Who are you?"

"Oh, Nic Cage. I'd shake your hand, but you're tied up."

"For real Nic Cage?"

"I suppose yes is the right answer to that question. Hold still."

Cage pulled a length of rope through a loop and freed Stanley's legs, then moved behind him to work on his wrists.

"I gave your girlfriend here a silver nitrate injection. Seared the curse right out of her and everyone else down the line who was infected."

"We're all cured?" Stanley asked. Cage popped in front of him again and smiled.

"Yeah, should be."

"You saved the world," Stanley said quietly. Cage looked at him thoughtfully for a moment.

"Probably best not to think about it," he suggested. He finished untying Stanley and stood up. Stanley got up as well, rubbing his wrists.

"What the hell just happened?"

"I was going to ask that about the dog. I mean, a dog? Did she bite the dog?" Cage asked. Stanley shrugged.

"I have no idea."

"Weirdest one yet," Cage said, shaking his head. He pulled out his phone and began texting someone.

"This has happened before?" Stanley asked. Cage held up a finger to silence him, then kept texting. He stopped and then a response notification came in. Then he typed another quick text and put his phone away.

"Sorry, what were you saying?"

"This has happened before?"

"Oh," Cage said. "No. Well, yes. Not often. From time to time. It's usually not a big deal."

"It's not a big deal?" Stanley asked, unsure how to take that news.

"Not really. I'll have my people take care of it. No one died, so that's a bonus. We'll say I was filming the movie here still, it'll be fine. You'll see."

Stanley opened his mouth and closed it again. What was he supposed to say to that?

"Listen, what's your name?"

"Stanley," he answered. Cage smiled, putting a hand on his shoulder.

"Listen, Stanley. Can I trust you with something since we both just watched a tiny me turn into a Maltese dog?"

"Is it a Maltese?" Stanley asked, looking back at Dog Cage.

"It is. I was cursed a while ago. A long while ago. So every so often, things go sideways and I accidentally infect a person. Your girl here was working First Aid on the set of my movie a week or so ago. I got banged up in a fight with Frank Grillo, and cut my lip. She must have scratched herself on my tooth or something when she was cleaning me up. It happens."

"Scratch herself on your tooth? Are you seriously Nic Cage?"

"Stanley, who do I look like? I'm sorry this happened. I truly am. If I'd known she was infected, I never would have left town. Then an outbreak happens when I'm in Bulgaria and it was just wild trying to get back here. You have no idea."

"Why are you a supernatural plague?" Stanley asked then. Cage's hand gripped his shoulder more tightly.

"I told you, Stanley. I was cursed. Long, long time ago. It's manageable, though. It's like cold sores. You just need to watch for outbreaks."

He pulled his hand away and held it out between them. Stanley took it and they shook.

"I have to go, Stanley. Lots of loose ends to tie up. I promise, though, everyone will be eager to forget this ever happened, you'll see. Given the choice between a WereCage outbreak and a film shoot that got out of hand, which one do you think people will believe?"

"Hey, WereCage was what I called them, too."

"Oh yeah? Great minds, Stanley."

Cage pointed at him and smiled, then turned and walked out of the apartment. Stanley looked down at Sara and sighed, getting to his knees next to her. He put his fingers on her neck and found her pulse strong and steady.

He closed her broken door over and sat down on the sofa with Dog Cage. It was a half hour before Sara woke up again, groggy and disoriented.

"I think you're going to be okay," Stanley told her. Her head whipped around, and she tried to focus her eyes on him.

"Stanley?" she asked. He was petting Dog Cage.

"Yeah. How do you feel?"

"What happened?"

"Nic Cage cured you. All of us, I guess."

She stared at him, exhaling loudly. It was not what she wanted to hear; he was sure.

"Are you sure? Maybe tomorrow -" she began. He pointed at the window. The moon was visible in the sky. Her body slumped, and she hung her head.

"Why are you still here?" she asked. He shrugged his shoulders.

"Wanted to make sure you were okay."

"Why? So you can gloat about saving the world?"

"Technically real Nic Cage saved the world. I think it was really him, anyway. I was tied to your chair."

She got to her feet unsteadily and looked at her broken door, then at Stanley.

"Just go," she said.

"Okay. I was just thinking, though, if you want, we can still get dinner."

She blinked, pursing her lips.

"You messing with me right now?" she asked. He shook his head.

"Why the hell would you want to go to dinner after all of that?"

"I dunno. Compare notes on what happened the last few days. We have a lot in common now, I think."

"You're trying to pick me up based on mutual lycanthropy? I was going to beat your head in with a baseball bat, Stanley."

"No, you weren't," he told her. "That was Cage. And I get it. Being Nic Cage is… intense. It's really intense."

"Yes, it is," she agreed. He shrugged.

"See? I'm right. Can't hold that against you. And it's still kind of early. I bet we can find a place that's open."

"You mean right now?" she said. He nodded.

"You are absolutely crazy, you know that?"

"We're not using that word," he told her.

"I guess not, huh? Alright."

He found Dog Cage's makeshift leash and slipped it over his head. They left the apartment together and headed out into the night, serenaded by the sound of more police sirens.

FIN